Dearest Camila,
Thank you for being
kind and caring all
the time. A true friend.
I hope you enjoy reading
my first book! xoxo

Laura
Rose-Mary

Yours Truly

LAURA ROSE-MARY

BookVenture Publishing LLC
1000 Country Lane Ste 300
Ishpeming MI 49849
www.bookventure.com
Hotline: 1(877) 276-9751
Fax: 1(877) 864-1686

Ordering Information:
Quantity sales. Special discounts are available on quantity purchases by corporations, associations, and others. For details, contact the publisher at the address above.

Printed in the United States of America.

Library of Congress Control Number	2018964330
ISBN-13: Softcover	978-1-64166-844-6
Pdf	978-1-64166-845-3
ePub	978-1-64166-846-0
Kindle	978-1-64166-847-7

Rev. date: 10/16/2018

My name is Abigail Melanie Mitchell. I don't really know how to start one of these… So here it goes.

First Entry:

My therapist told me I should keep a journal, that it would help me get over this. Ha. 'Get over it,' like it's just a flu that I'll get over it in a few days… No. Not going to happen. Not even close.

I'm depressed. I have depression. Not a stomach flu. Depression.

The Merriam-Webster dictionary defines depression as;

a) A state of feeling sad

b) A serious medical condition in which a person feels very sad, hopeless, and unimportant and often is unable to live a normal way

To live a normal way… What the hell does that even mean?

Ha. These people probably never even spoken to a person with depression before… Because if they did… Well, they would know. Everyone would know. It's not about being sad all the time, it's so much more than that. So much more… I mean, don't get me wrong that is a part of it, but it's not the whole thing. You'll never really understand unless you've lived with it. And I don't mean someone you know has had it. I mean, you have experienced it for yourself. You need to know the pain behind it to really understand… I guess that's my problem. No one understands.

Do you know what it is like to not be able to move? I don't mean you're stuck somewhere and can't move because something heavy is on you and you don't have the strength to pick it up yourself... I mean being alone in your room, laying on your bed, stuck, unable to move, because you are trapped... trapped. In your mind. Nothing is actually holding you back or on top of you so you can't move. It's your mind, it's all in your mind.

That's what it's like. To be depressed. For me.

Well a part of it...

Ugh. But who am I kidding. No one is ever going to read this. So why should I even bother to write in this stupid journal? Because a snobby therapist told me to? When she doesn't really care about me... She doesn't really 'understand' me, even though she keeps saying she does. She's never been through what I've been through. So she doesn't actually know. No one does.

Screw this. This is so pointless.

At least I can say that I tried it. Ha. Screw you Ms. Stupid Therapist.

Yours Truly,

Abigail Mitchell

So, it's me again. I told my therapist that I tried to write in this journal but it was pointless, but she made me promise her that I would try one more time. So WOHOO here I am.

I don't really know what I should talk about…

Well, okay, so I know I told you what it's like to have depression, but that's not the only kind of depression. It's different for everybody.

I learned that from this group my parents are making me go to. This girl a year younger than me has Manic Depression, well now they call it Bipolar Disorder. Which really sucks, because you can go from being in a happy mood and 0.5 seconds later get upset and depressed, and then go back to being happy 5 minutes after that… weird. She has to take medication everyday called 'lithium'. It's supposed to balance out your mood swings to keep you under control. I… I feel so bad for her.

I don't know what I would do if I couldn't control myself.

I tried another attempt today… I took a knife from the kitchen and went upstairs and sat in the bathtub. Right before I was going to cut my wrists… I stopped. Hesitated and I thought of that girl. I closed my eyes and saw her sitting across from me smiling. She said something but I couldn't quite hear her. But I could see her smiling, I could see that she has dimples, I've never seen them before, and she smiled at me for a long time. I tried to talk but I couldn't. I felt trapped again, but I felt happy. I was happy because she was smiling at me.

Something happened to me today, and I can't really explain it. For once I was actually happy, I was happy to be alive, and I was happy to have met that girl.

I think she just saved my life...

I don't even know her name. But I remember her face vividly. Long blonde straight hair, chubby cheeks, dimples, braces, a cute bunny like nose, big green eyes, perfectly shaped eyebrows and a small forehead. She looks like a sweet girl, you wouldn't think just looking at her that she has Manic Depression. Which kind of makes me wonder who else has it... I wonder how many people in the world have depression. There are so many different kinds of depressions, and now that I think of it... Everyone in the group that I go to look 'normal'. They look like the average person you'd see on the side walk waiting for the bus or at the mall on boxing day. Which is very interesting to me. Because we all look 'normal' but once a 'normal' person finds out that you have whatever kind of depression... You become a 'freak'. I just don't get it...

Well, I guess that's all I really have to say.

I'm thankful for that girl today, without her I wouldn't of been able to write this. And to be totally honest, this isn't really that bad... Writing in the journal I mean.

Yours Truly,

Abigail Mitchell

Third Entry:

Some days I feel like I have nowhere to turn, yet I have the whole world at my finger tips. I feel like I'm trapped, with nowhere to go, but I can see the door wide open in front of me. I feel things, a lot of things, but some days… I can't feel anything at all. Those days are the worst days.

Those days, when I don't feel anything at all, are the days I try… I give up, I want to end things because I think that nothing can be worse than not feeling anything at all.

But, I see her face now…

It's been two weeks since I've tried. That's a record. I'm actually really proud of myself.

I really wish I knew who that girl was, because I'd thank her like there's no tomorrow. Something about her touched me, and I want her to know that. Maybe if she knew then she wouldn't be down as often as she used to, because I know I'm not. I want to help her. I've never wanted to help anyone before, because well, I felt like no one has ever wanted to help me. They just sent me to see a psych that doesn't actually care about her patients, she just does it for the paychecks.

I feel like I have a different outlook on things now. I've done some research on Manic Depression or Bipolar Disorder, just to know what she goes through. It's a lot different then what I thought…

I almost feel like I'm not even depressed compared to her. I don't take medications, I don't go from happy to sad to angry back to happy in the span of 10 minutes. I'm just down all the time.

But I guess, like I said before, there's so many different types of depression, and yes, all of them suck.

I feel like I'm drowning in my own mind. I can hear every single thought that goes through my brain every single day and I don't know how to stop it. I hear people say things like, "I didn't think about it I just did it. I cleared my mind and just jumped." … How is that possible? I wish I knew how to clear my mind…

Well I guess I know how, but I can't go down that path again because all I see is those bright green eyes, long blonde hair, braces and dimples, smiling at me.

I hear what she's saying now.

"Remember you are loved."

And that's it… "Remember you are loved"… Loved by who? My parents? HAHA not likely, they couldn't care less, I mean if they actually cared, why would they send me back to the same therapist…

Well… Maybe they do, maybe they actually love me… I never really thought about it before, but underneath it all they just don't know how to cope. Maybe I am loved… hm. Never thought of it that way…

Yours Truly,

Abigail Mitchell

Fourth Entry:

It's been a while since I've written in this. Sorry.

But things have been different lately. It's like my family somehow have learned to accept me.

They care… They actually care.

But, I don't know… It's too much, I think. I'm definitely not used to this. At all. And to be honest, I can't help but question it all…

> Do they really care? Like honestly care? If so, why now? Why all of a sudden?
> What changed their minds?

I keep going back to the meetings every Saturday morning, just to see that girl. But it's been over a month now, and I haven't seen her since that first day. And I'm kind of scared… Who knows what happened to her, or maybe she's okay now. I don't know. I just wish I could see her, even for five minutes.

Just to say thank you.

***

So, um, I met a guy the other day.

He was at one of my meetings. I went on Wednesday to see if that girl maybe switched days, but she wasn't at that one either. But he was. He was there with his little sister.

His eyes. They were simply, complex and they had this sparkle to them, something I've never seen before.

His name is Dylan.

He was wearing this grey t-shirt with a black lion on it. And it stood out to me, but I don't know why. Then his sister started to talk, and she went on to say how lion's are her all time favourite animal. How they're always so strong and she wishes she could be like them one day. Like her brother.

It was so wonderful to see him there to support his little sister. I mean none of my family ever comes to these meetings. They say they're the best but they can't take twenty minutes out of their days just to sit with me and listen, for once. But Dylan goes. Every week. That's amazing! Honestly amazing.

I'm going to my meeting tomorrow, I told him that's when I usually go. And he said, "If my sister's up to it, we'll be there." I was in shock. This guy was going to come to another boring meeting just to see me again.

I don't know what it is lately, but I'm kind of thinking… Life really isn't too bad.

Yours Truly,

Abigail Mitchell

It's me again. I went to my meeting on Saturday… No green eyed girl and no Dylan.

Why do I do this to myself? I get so excited over stupid things and end up just getting disappointed. This is so dumb. Plus, I have to go to my therapist tomorrow… Ugh. I don't want to go! She doesn't understand me or anyone else at her practice probably, ha.

She's going to ask about this journal and I don't know what to say about it. I mean, it's not that bad, but it's stupid at the same time. So what I met this green eyed girl at my first meeting and haven't seen her since. I met this seems to be amazing guy named Dylan, and he said he'd come to the meeting Saturday if he could, but he didn't. Maybe it was something to do with his sister, but I don't know.

I'm so stupid. I should of asked that girl what her name was. I should of asked Dylan for his phone number to see if he'd be coming to the meeting so I wouldn't get my hopes up for nothing. I even wore a dress… A dress! I haven't worn a dress since I was like ten years old.

It's just like I see so much possibility in new people. Like they won't know me, so they won't judge me right off the bat. They could actually get to know the real me. Abigail Melanie Mitchell. Not "the freak Abi who thinks she's depressed." Ugh I hate people at my school. I just want something new. Something that's not going to disappoint me anymore.

Speaking of disappointments… I'm pretty sure my parents just see me as a big disappointment.

But jeez, so are they. I mean, they're not doing a good job at keeping their youngest daughter happy. It's like they don't really care about me. It seemed like they did, for about a week. But then of course, it was all just for a stupid family gathering. They wanted all of us to go to and me not to be boring me, for me to put on an act that I live in a happy family, that I'm a happy girl and my parents aren't actually fighting.

Did I tell you that yet?

Well, my parents fight all the time. And they think I don't notice, but come on it's pretty obvious. My room is down the other end of the hall from theirs and I can still hear them yelling at each other. It's happening more often now, too. Before it just used to be an occasional thing. But now… Now it's a weekly thing, a few times a week sometimes.

It's like they think I'm stupid, that just because I'm depressed that I still have the brain of a five year old. No. I'm almost seventeen. And I'm not an idiot. I'm actually pretty smart for my age, my teachers think so too. But no matter how much I tell my parents, and show them my grades, they still don't care. And I'm really getting sick and tired of it. How can you not care about your daughter's school grades? That she's actually third in her class. All you care is that she's depressed… And being depressed, isn't normal. So they think their daughter is just a freak. I bet they wish they never had me. Well me too. Sometimes I wish they hadn't…

Yours Truly,

Abigail Mitchell

Sixth Entry:

Oh. My. God. If I didn't hate my therapist enough already.

Now I have to do this journaling thing daily. Why? Because she doesn't think it's helping me enough. Um… If it's not working now what makes you think it's going to work more by forcing me to do it daily.

And get this.

I have to be supervised while I write…. To ensure that it happens every day and it's at least one page. I wish I could change the font size to 72, then I'd be done so fast and I could go eat some pizza. HA, omg I crack myself up sometimes.

But in all seriousness… T H I S S U C K S !

Good thing is the person watching me doesn't actually have to read this. So I actually could just talk about random stuff for a page and they'd never know it! But now that I think about it, she'll probably look at this at some point, so I guess I could try.

Soooooooooooooooooooooooooooo…

I'm debating whether or not to go to the Wednesday meeting tomorrow. Dylan might be there again. But who knows. Maybe he lied and he actually doesn't go every Wednesday, and he only said that to impress me. But jeez, if he was trying to impress me, why didn't he show up Saturday? I guess it could have been something to do with his sister… Oh jeez, I hope she's okay.

I hope that other girl is okay too. I still wish I could see her. I just want to know her name, I want to thank her, I want her to know what she's done for me and I want to know how she's doing. I did all that research on Bipolar Disorder, but I want to know her take on it.

Ew… her take on it? Gross, I sound like my therapist.

Okay, let me try this again… I want to know how she's feeling and what it's like to be Bipolar. I'm curious, maybe we have similarities or we might just be extremely different people. But I'll never know unless I can see her again.

I just don't understand how she can just disappear like that…

I really hope she goes tomorrow or Saturday. I just need to see her.

Wish me luck. I'm going to need it.

Yours Truly,

Abigail Mitchell

I'm so nervous! I'm just having a snack before I go to my meeting and I don't know what to expect. Maybe I shouldn't expect anything because then I won't get disappointed right? Yeah, but I want them to be there. I want to see that cute green eyed girl, I want to see Dylan again, and surprisingly I want to see everyone else. It's kind of weird but I don't mind going to these meetings, because I get to learn about so many different kinds of depressions. It's actually fascinating to me.

Okay, okay! I'm going to go now and I promise, as soon as I get home I'll write in here to tell you how it all went! I feel good about today! I really hope everyone is there.

***

Is it possible to fall in love at first sight and second and third?!

I saw Dylan today! He looked even better then I remembered. He apologized for not being able to come sooner. His mother is sick. Wow. First his sister, and now his mom. I don't know how he handles all of it. He's so strong. I can see why his sister loves him so much. He wore another lion shirt today too. I find it adorable actually.

That girl wasn't there, again. But… Dylan said he's seen her before and he'd give me her number because his little sister and that girl have hung-out before. This is so exciting! I can't remember the last time I've actually looked forward to something. He's going to call me tomorrow with her number.

I learned about another kind of depression today. Dylan's little sister Lexi. She has Psychotic Depression. She has the same symptoms of Major Depression, but she goes through some more symptoms with this kind of depression and they are: hallucinations, delusions and/or paranoia. And she has to take a combination of antidepressant and antipsychotic medications to treat her depression. Because it's a combination of the two medications she has to be watched all the time. I guess that's why her brother and her are so close. But wow, this is crazy. She's only 11 years old and she suffers from this.

Doing all this research about other people's depression made me wonder if mine actually had a name. And it does. I have all the symptoms for Major Depression, or as my doctor calls it "Major Depressive Disorder." And some of the symptoms are: -trouble going to sleep at night -feeling like things around you are either speeding up or slowing down -being tired a lot and not having energy -feeling worthless -troubles concentrating -hard time making decisions -suicidal thoughts, etc.

I could take antidepressant medication, but my parents still think this is just a phase, like I said before, a flu I'll get over soon. But it's not. I feel worthless all the time, and trapped. Those are my two main ones. Then because of those I get suicidal thoughts because I just want all of it to end, then at least I'd feel something besides numbness.

I wish I was 18, then I could take whatever medication I wanted. I wish I wasn't depressed. I wish I had parents that cared. I wish someone would just love me. I mean, I don't ask for much. Please. Anyone…

Yours Truly,

Abigail Mitchell

Eighth Entry:

Guess what! Dylan called!!

I thought his voice was attractive in person… but on the phone, OH MY GOOD GOD. I wanted to ask him to marry me after the first two minutes. But, I didn't. Ha! I wish I did though. Anyways, we talked for what seemed like hours! There's something so beautiful and comforting in his voice. I don't really know how to describe it, but, it was amazing. We talked about so many different things, and I wasn't scared at all. I mean, like I'm always nervous to open up to people because I think it's just useless and pointless because they don't actually care about you they just pretend to just to know your secrets. But I talked to him with such ease! I was honestly proud of myself. He asked if we could get a coffee tomorrow. And, I said yes!

Omg…

I just realized… I've never actually been on a date before. Not like this is a date, because he didn't really say it was a date, but it is just going to be the two of us and no one else, and we're going for coffee and we can sit in the corner and talk, hold hands maybe… Kiss maybe… OMG. Oh my goodness! Kiss? My first date AND my first kiss?! I don't know if I can handle both in one day!

Another problem!! What am I going to wear?! I mean, I wore my favourite dress to my last meeting, but he didn't show up so technically he didn't see me in it! But what if we take a picture together then people from the meeting might see the picture and then they think I'm weird and only own one dress…

The things that go on in my head, OMG. But jeez, who cares what they think, right? I'm just happy to be going for coffee with Dylan!

Actually, I know exactly what I'm going to wear. My favourite jeans, and a nice shirt. Casual. Because that's how I usually dress, I shouldn't have to dress up for him if he liked what he saw in the first place, right? Yeah! That's what I think at least.

Oh my gosh! I almost forgot to tell you! So Dylan also gave me that girl's number. Her name is Alexandria. What a beautiful name! I sent her a text so hopefully she gets it and replies soon!

I really hope she likes me. I hope she can hangout, as soon as possible. Even just for an ice cream for like twenty minutes. I want to thank her so much. I want her to know how she has helped me. I still think sometimes in cutting myself again, but before I even go to get something sharp I already stop myself. And I hear in the back of my mind, "Remember you are loved."

I'm kind of really starting to like this journaling thing. It's like I have someone to talk to who won't judge me. I just wish you could talk back to me. Because now I'm getting nervous... I'm having a coffee date with a BOY, and I finally got in contact with Alexandria! Two people that I can't wait to be a part of my life. Because I feel like they will understand me and I'll actually, finally have some friends! But there's that chance they won't like me and both will be one time things, and I'll just got back to being Abi the Freak...

Ugh, I've got to stop doubting everything and just have an open mind with no expectations...

Wish me luck!

Yours Truly,

Abigail Mitchell

It's a gorgeous Friday afternoon and I'm getting ready for my date!!! I'm so excited! I have a date in less than an hour! Did I mention I'm kind of excited?! For my date? Well… I am! Okay, okay! I better go an finish doing my hair before it's time for my date!

Wish me luck! I'll tell you all about it as soon as I get back!

SO excited!

***

Hello! I'm back!

I had the most perfect time! We both had a coffee and the same kind of doughnut. Come on! It's totally fate. Like totally. Ha!

Anyways, we sat and talked for two hours straight. No awkwardness or weirdness at all! He has two sisters. Lexi his younger sister that I met, and another one who's older and in college, her name is Lilly. His parents are still together, his dad works at a law office in town and his mom is as stay at home mom. But now she's in the hospital for chemotherapy. I feel so bad for her. Their family is so beautiful, and so strong. I mean like wow! First Lexi and now their mother. That's crazy…

The way he spoke about his family was so beautiful, he really loves them and I can tell they love him too. I'm actually kind of jealous of him… I have an older brother and sister, but they both moved out and are never around, and my parents still fight all the time. His family gets along so well, and when they have arguments they always talk things out like normal people… Instead of my family that just ignores each other until one person gives in and apologies with some kind of expensive gift.

When will my family understand that you can't buy happiness? Its cliché but I don't care. It's true! Maybe that's one reason why I get so down all the time. They just try to buy me things to "cheer me up" and get over this "flu." Omg, they're never going to understand me. I wish I was a part of their family. Mine sucks.

Oh! On a brighter note, Alexandria replied to me! She's going to do her best to go to the meeting tomorrow and then we're going to go to the mall after. It's only a couple blocks away from the church and my Mom said she'd pick me up after she got off work. So this is perfect!

I'm so excited to finally see her again. I really hope she can come tomorrow. I have so much I want to say to her… I should probably write them all down before I forget. Ah! I hope she likes me, and I hope she doesn't think I'm weird… OMG. What if she thinks I'm weird when I tell her I keep seeing her face and hear her voice say, "Remember you are loved," before I try to cut myself…

Why, why, why do I over think everything… How do I know if I should tell Alexandria everything tomorrow or not? Ugh… Wish me luck, I guess…

Yours Truly,

Abigail Mitchell

Tenth Entry:

Wow, what an eventful day. I don't even know where I should begin…

I barely slept because I was so excited, and when I did actually sleep I had these weird dreams, and I didn't like them at all. I saw Alexandria, Lexi and Dylan in this room. They were sitting on these chairs, silent. I tried to talk to them but I couldn't say anything, I could move my lips but no sound would come out. I felt trapped. I haven't felt trapped in a while… Then I saw the three of them just sitting there laughing and smiling. I couldn't hear them either. I was trapped inside this box, all four sides were glass and there was no way out. I didn't know what to do, and I started to freak out, and then I woke up. I got a glass of water and went back to bed. As soon as I fell back asleep I was back in that glass box. But this time I was alone. I couldn't see anything, it was all white. I tried screaming for help and this time I could actually speak, but there was no one around to hear me. I just kept screaming and screaming as loud as I could for what seemed like forever, hoping someone would come by to help me out of this box…

All of a sudden I woke up, and I had a razor blade in my hand. I don't know how I got it, but I had it in my hand. Then the pain started to kick in… I did my thighs and left wrist. Luckily they weren't too deep and I was able to bandage myself up in the bathroom before anyone else woke up…

I don't know how I got that razor blade, or how I cut myself in my sleep, but do I know I'm scared... Just when things seem to be getting better, something always happens to me. I relapse. I hate it. I wish I had more strength, but I don't. I wish I had someone to look out for me all the time, like Dylan does with Lexi, but I don't. I wish I had someone who cared enough about me to help, but I don't.

I was really nervous to go to the meeting after waking up like that...

I spent all morning in my room. I didn't talk to anyone. I was devastated, I didn't know what to do. My siblings are home for the weekend and my parents are both in town for once on the same weekend, but I couldn't face them all. I knew it would just add another layer of disappointment they already have with me. I'm a failure. It's like I'm addicted to cutting myself and I can't stop. I mean I did for a while, but it went away. Fast. I mean real fast. Like honestly since I woke up I feel like a different person. I have no confidence in myself anymore. I don't believe I can do anything, I feel worthless and I feel numb. I feel numb all over. Man, I don't know what to do. I'm only sixteen, why do I have to feel like this?

I called Emotions Anonymous (the meetings I go to) to find out who was going to be leading the meeting today so that maybe I could talk with them before or after, privately. They said the meeting at my church was canceled for today, because some illness came up in the leaders family, and they couldn't get anyone else in on such short notice, but they are going to have a makeup meeting on Monday evening for those who usually go on Saturdays.

Ok. That was fine, I guess. Things like that happen once and a while. No problem...

Problem for me though. I was scared when I was in my dreams, I was scared when I woke up and I've been scared ever since and I need someone to talk to but I don't know who I could talk to about this.

My siblings are here, yes, but they wouldn't understand and I'm pretty sure they probably wouldn't really care because they're never around here anymore anyways. My parents are still in bed, probably hung over from some fancy party last night, and even if they were fine, I still probably wouldn't talk to them because they definitely don't care at all.

I haven't met up with Alexandria yet, so it would probably be weird if I just texted her about my dream, so I probably shouldn't do that.

Dylan is probably at the hospital this morning with Lexi, visiting their mom. They usually go every Saturday morning really early with breakfast for their mom, then they all sit on her bed and watch cartoons together. It's really quite sweet actually.

UGH! I have no one to talk to. Don't get me wrong, I'm really liking journaling, but I need to talk to someone who can actually talk back. Yes, it feels great to write all my feelings and thoughts down and get them all off my chest, but right now I need something more. I need someone to listen to me and actually care… I just don't know what to do!

***

So I went to the mall around 2PM because we usually get out of the meetings around that time anyways. I was hoping Alexandria would be there. But I didn't see her. We said we would meet at the entrance to the food court. I waited for almost an hour. Which was fine because I brought some homework with me, and I got most of it done anyway. I was packing up my bag and I looked up and saw Alexandria. I almost yelled! I was so happy to see her.

She looked exactly how I remembered her, long blonde hair, cute chubby cheeks, and big green eyes. She was beautiful. You know, It still amazes me how 'normal' all of us depressed people look. You would never know if someone was depressed just by looking at them. I guess it is true, don't judge a book by its cover.

Anyways, Alexandria sat with me and we talked for a while. Just about casual things, like school and boys. She was happy to know that I went on a date with Dylan. She knows that family very well, and thinks Dylan and I would make a cute couple. (I do to!)

After we kind of ran out of general topics I thought it was time to talk about more serious stuff. I asked her what it's like living with Bipolar Disorder. She was really open and honest about it and it really made me connect with her on a whole other level. It's not that I go through the exact same things as her, it's just like the same kind of feelings sometimes. When she was done, I asked her if I could be honest with her about something, and she said, "Yeah of course." So I said, "Please don't take this the wrong way or anything, but your face has stopped me from cutting myself. I mean like, I tried a while ago and when I shut my eyes, you popped up and I had to stop. And then I heard you tell me something. And you said, "Remember you are loved." And I was so confused… but it helped me. You helped me a lot. I guess what I'm just trying to say is, Thank you."

She looked up at me with tears in her eyes and said, "No please. Thank you. You've helped me more then you know."

I was in shock. I helped her? I actually helped someone? I'm not actually useless? I can't believe it…

Yours Truly,

Abigail Mitchell

Eleventh Entry:

I went to church this morning. I used to go all the time when I was younger, but my parents stopped taking me once they started fighting. They couldn't agree on things anymore, so they just stopped doing almost everything we used to do.

I guess that's maybe where this all started. My depression. My parents triggered it, I think…

Back to the church thing. I went to confession and honestly I feel lighter. I still feel really bad about yesterday and I told the Priest that and he said The Lord forgave me, and that it was time to forgive myself too…

But the thing is, I don't really know how to forgive myself. I cut myself without even knowing I did it. Waking up to a razor blade in your hand is a very scary feeling… Who knows what could of happened if I didn't wake up then. What if I was asleep for five more minutes? I might of actually committed suicide without even wanting to. That's really scary to me. Well I'm sure it would be to anyone.

You know, I finally realized that I don't want to die. I don't want to cut myself just to feel something other than numbness. I'm happy with who I am, so I shouldn't have to change that in any way.

But now I'm afraid to sleep… Because I'm afraid I'll wake up with more damage to my body. I don't want to be depressed anymore, I don't want to feel numb anymore, and I don't want to be afraid of myself. I really am afraid and I don't know what to do. I want to tell someone. I really do, I just don't know who…

I have an appointment with my therapist tomorrow (just like every other Monday.) I feel like I should tell her. But if I tell her, she's probably going to tell my parents, and I don't want them to find out. I don't want anyone to find out because I was doing so well. I really thought I was doing well, and then this happened. And the worst part is that I didn't mean for it to actually happen. But I guess it's kind of a sign, in a weird way. Like my subconscious is telling me maybe I'm not making all the progress that I actually think I'm making.

Now I want to know why I did it. If it was a sign then that means something is going on inside me that I need to figure out in order to get through this. I guess I should talk about it tomorrow. I mean it feels good talking about it here, but this journal can't help me. It just is a way for me to express myself without judgment.

I really like journaling now.

So I guess I should learn to like my therapist to.

Well maybe not like her exactly, but the idea of talking out loud about what is going on inside me. Because writing it all out helps, but I'm pretty sure talking about it might help even more…

Ugh, wish me luck for tomorrow. I'm going to need it.

Yours Truly,

Abigail Mitchell

Twelfth Entry:

Hi, it's me. Well who else would it be haha.

Sooooo, I'm in the hospital… I'm okay! Just here for a checkup, because like I said she probably would, my therapist told my parents and so now I'm here. I got two stitches on both thighs and my left wrist is just bandaged up. They weren't too bad of cuts. I was lucky.

So you probably realized I told my therapist everything, and I did. I honestly didn't really mind it. I think because this time was different. I've realized a lot since I first started going to see my therapist and going to the EA meetings.

Everyone is different and goes through life in a different way. You could grow up with the same group of people and go to school with them, but never really know them…

For example, I saw a guy from my homeroom class, in the hospital. He was there on a suicide attempt too. Except his was on purpose. I never would of thought, to see him there. Or anyone from my school actually. It's crazy to think about. He's this popular guy, everyone knows him and wants to be his friend. I used to have a crush on him in grade 4. But then he started hanging out with the popular people and forgot about me and everyone else who wasn't as popular, and he changed. I wonder why he would try to take his life… It seems like his life is perfect, but I guess it's really not what it seems.

This brings me back to my thoughts before about how people look normal and you could never tell who is depressed, and then once a 'normal' person finds out there's something off about you they call you names and treat you differently. I find this so dumb. Why can't people treat people with the same amount of respect? I mean, I don't treat people differently because I'm depressed. In fact, I try to treat them as best as I can, to make them laugh and smile… Because to be honest, I know what it's like to be down all the time. It really sucks, and I honestly don't want anyone else to feel like that, ever.

Dylan and Lexi stopped by. It was super sweet. Lexi made me a get well soon card, and Dylan gave me a small stuffed animal of a lion. Of course. He said Lexi picked it out. They stayed with me for a couple hours, and we played some cards and watched some TV. Dylan held my hand while we watched it. I kind of freaked (on the inside, of course!)

Alexandria called, too. She couldn't make it before visiting hours were over, which was okay, so she said she would come over to my house tomorrow when I got home. She said she had a gift for me too.

Wow. It's amazing to think about all the people who care about me now. Maybe they always have and just never knew how to show it properly. But then again I don't think there's just one 'proper' way. Also, it could be me, I feel like I'm changing. I'm realizing a lot, I'm learning a lot, and I'm growing up a lot.

I'm thankful for the people I have in my life. I'm learning to accept myself for who I am, and be grateful for it. I'm grateful for a lot.

I'm glad I opened up today. And I think that I'm on a pretty good path now.

Yours Truly,

Abigail Mitchell

Thirteenth Entry:

I got out of the hospital this morning, but I didn't go to school today. I stayed home and so did my parents. They stayed with me. They took care of me. I actually had a pretty good day. I mean after we got through the pity party, it was actually sweet.

We went through old photo albums and laughed.

My mother and I baked, while my dad played his guitar. I haven't heard my dad play in so long.

My birthday is next week, and they said they were going to throw me a big party. But honestly… I don't really want one. I mean I have no one to invite and I'm not one for big fancy parties anyways.

I told them that, and I think they were okay with it.

They actually listened to me.

They're going to invite Dylan and Lexi, and Alexandria over and if there's anyone else I wanted. I'm kind of thinking about inviting James. The popular guy I told you about that I saw in the hospital. I don't even know if he'll show up, but I mean it's worth a shot.

We're going to have a sundae bar and popcorn maker with all the seasonings you can think of, and we're going to have a movie marathon in the back yard. My parents just got this new projector screen it's like over one hundred inches! Cool, right? And we can watch whatever movies we want and eat all the junk food in the world.

I'm really looking forward to it!

Another good note! Alex came over for a while today. She brought me a card and a stuffed animal of a puppy. It was so cute and it had big green eyes just like her. She also opened up to me again, This time it was how I helped her.

I've told you before that Alex has Manic Depression (Bipolar Disorder). Well here's the thing, there's a percentage of people with this depression that suffer from substance abuse problems as well as the bipolar depression. So, because of the craziness of the mood swings and then the depression adding on to that, bipolar people are more likely to turn to taking drugs or alcohol to try to help and manage their symptoms of their disorder... Alex is one of those people. She got into some of her parents prescription medication at home and she overdosed and went to the hospital. That's why I didn't see her for so long. She was getting treatments done and she was in a teenage rehab facility.

But, Alex didn't know she took the wrong medications. She took them by accident and no one believed her. No one asked her why she took the medication, they just assumed the worst things. Poor girl. She wasted over a month of her life trying to convince everyone she didn't mean to do it. That she was really okay and it was a honest mistake. But because she's bipolar her mind plays tricks on her sometimes and she started to really believe that she purposely did the damage to herself.

That's when she told me how I helped her...

She heard this voice in her head. She didn't know exactly who's it was, but it sounded familiar.

Well…

It was me.

All through the rehabilitation she heard my voice. Alex said, "I would hear so many different things. Stuff like how if I kept doing good I could finally go home. If I just keep pushing myself I could leave."

Of course I've never said these things before, but it was my voice in her head saying them. It was like she was trying to say the things she needed to hear but because it was her own voice she didn't really care that much to try to get out because no one believed her anyways, so why keep trying? But then the thoughts changed to my voice. And she couldn't figure out who's voice it was. And I guess because she wanted to know the voice so bad, that was her motivation to finally listen and get herself out of there.

Her parents believe her now. It was a honest mistake.

Her mom had some old infection prescription behind the mirror in the main bathroom upstairs and just forgot to throw out the bottle when she was done. There were a few pills left into it. Alex thought they were hers because she was almost done her bottle too. Alex forgot that she moved her bottle to her night stand in her bedroom the day before because she was angry that her parents didn't give her enough space in that bathroom so she moved half her stuff into her room. Now because she was in one of her mood swings she forgot half of what she moved because she says sometimes when she has a mood swing it's so much for her that she blacks out for a bit until she calms back down.

Alex forgot.

It really was a mistake. Just like me cutting myself the other day.

Alex and I kind of have a lot in common, but we're also very different. We have our different kinds of depressions as a common ground. But I can tell she's so much more than her depression. And so am I.

We both could have bright futures. I can see us being friends for the rest of our lives.

Okay, this might be kind of cheesy… But I don't care. I'm excited to see what life has to offer me. Because life really isn't as shitty as what I thought it was for a while.

My principal called my house today.

He spoke with my parents.

My mom told me Mr. Thomson wants me to speak at the next school assembly, only if it was one hundred percent okay with me of course. He said there's a lot of students at my school that are going through similar things that I am. He said that I could make a difference in their lives. He said that he would talk more with me when I came back to school. He said to take all the time I needed to heal, and I'll be able to start back to school when I was ready and only when I was.

People are really starting to show they care… And you know what? I love it! I love them, and I'm learning to love myself. Just the way I am.

Yours Truly,

Abigail Mitchell

Fourteenth Entry:

Alex and I went to the EA meeting together today. It was a lot of fun. It's so cool to finally have a friend that knows what I'm going through. Even though she's not going through the exact same things as me, but she has a better understanding than most people. It's no pity party. It's two girls hanging out as if we were normal and there was nothing wrong with us. Sometimes I think there isn't anything wrong with us. And that we're going to be just fine. Together. As best friends.

I learnt about yet another kind of depression today. This one is called Seasonal Affective Disorder.

This guy got up to talk today for the first time. I've seen him at meetings before. I honestly just thought maybe he was someone's friend that just shows up for support. But he's depressed too. He has S.A.D. That's when light affects your emotions. Like for example, it's always darker in the winter time and that's when he's most down. When it's winter he has to sit in front of this light box for at least an hour each day, sometimes a couple times a day and it's like sitting out in the sun. It's supposed to help brighten up their mood. He also has to take antidepressants with the light therapy. And in the seasons like the spring and summer he's 'okay'. Just the odd rainy days he has to sit in front of the light box.

That's so crazy to think that during the year in the spring and summer and going into fall you could be this okay and 'normal' person, but as soon as the weather really starts to change and the sun isn't out as often, you get depressed and have to take medications and sit in front of a light box daily for light therapy. Imagine thinking you're fine and making progress in your life and that you're actually doing great, and then the weather changes and you're right back to square one.

On another note, I'm also going on a date with Dylan tomorrow. He's going to pick me up at my house and take me to dinner and a movie! I'm so excited! But like so nervous. This is my second date with him and I hope it goes well. I really like Dylan, and I hope he feels the same way.

I spoke to my parents about what my principle said… I don't think I'm going to do it. It's too soon for me I think. I'd love to help other people, but I don't think I'll be much help when I did, you know, what I did last week.

I'm on a good path right now, and I want to keep it that way. Maybe one day I'll have the courage to speak in front of people and help them. I really do feel like I could help someone. I mean I did, Alex. And now we're are best friends. It feels really good, knowing that I've helped someone. I want to help more, I really do. I just need a little more time.

I read a quote today, I don't know who it's by:

"Stars can't shine without darkness."

As cheesy as it sounds, I want to be a star one day. I've been through all the darkness I can handle in one life time. It's time for me to start shining, like a star.

Yours Truly,

Abigail Mitchell

Fifteenth Entry:

Sooooo, I'm getting ready for my date and I'm super early and I figured I'd tell you about my day so far. I stayed home again today. My dad had to go to work, but my mom stayed home with me.

My mom asked me how I was feeling. I think this is the first time she's actually genuinely asked me that. I didn't really know how to answer at first. Eventually I said, "I'm feeling better each day. I was really scared Saturday morning and I wanted to tell you but it was too difficult. I'm glad I finally did though. It feels good to know that I have people that care and are actually showing it."

My mom was silent. I didn't know what to do. After a while she finally spoke. She said, " I've wanted to help you Abi my love. I just never knew how. It broke my heart to hear what you did without evening know it. I was right down the hall. I could have been there for you. I should have been there for you. I should have known."

My mom and I sat in silence on the couch and just hugged. I could feel her regret and it broke my heart. We cried, then somehow laughed and now I feel good. I mean, I'm not at one hundred percent yet. But I'm on the way there. I'm making progress and that's all that matters.

Oh my gosh!

Dylan is going to be here in like fifteen minutes and I'm not done my hair yet! I have to go! But don't worry, I'll journal about the date as soon as I get home!

Wish me luck!

***

I'm back! I had the most terrific time. I swear it was like magical!

Dylan is just so great and I can't get enough! It's like we were meant to meet each other. It's cheesy but I don't care! Some people are just meant to be together. Yes, I know I'm only sixteen but I turn seventeen in like a week! But I still don't care! Love is love no matter who you are or what age. Some people say there's love at first sight and I believe in it. I used to hate all those love songs I hear on the radio, but now I turn the volume up and sing along.

I know this might be crazy but I really don't care. My life is finally changing for the better and I'm here for the ride. No way do I ever want to go back.

I've got nothing but good things ahead of me.

I have scars from my cuts, but that's all they are. Scars. In the past.

I've got a bright future and I'm ready for it.

Yours Truly,

Abigail Mitchell

Sixteenth Entry:

Sorry I haven't written in like a week! I've been super busy.

I had my Seventeenth Birthday party yesterday. It was so much fun! All my friends were there. It was really fun! Nothing too fancy just a lot of junk food, jokes and scary movies!

I also went on another date with Dylan! It was a couple days before my birthday and we went for ice cream. It was really sweet. And I don't just mean the ice cream!

Guess what!

Dylan asked me to be his girlfriend, oh my gosh, it was so great! And of course I remember every word he said! He said, "I know we've only gone on a couple dates so far, and trust me I'm going to take you on a lot more. But… I'd like to take you on those dates as my girlfriend. Before you say anything, there's more! I know you don't see it, but I do… You are one beautiful and remarkable girl Abigail and there is nowhere else in this world I'd rather be then right by your side. I know you're figuring out who you are and you are doing one hell of a job. And I am loving every minute of it. So I hope that you feel the same way, and want to continue to grow… Together. As boyfriend and girlfriend. Soo, what do you think?"

Well duh! I said, "Yes!"

It's such a cool feeling to have a boyfriend. I don't think I'll ever get tired of hearing it, or saying it! Hey did I mention I have a boyfriend now?! Yay!

School is almost out for the summer and I can't wait! I got a part time job at the ice cream shop near my house. I think it'll be fun to work there!

I also talked to my therapist about the idea of helping people. There's this camp for kids and teenagers with depression. It happens every summer, for two weeks in August. And I'm going to go to it! I'm going to be one of the councilors. I don't really know what to expect. But I'm learning not to expect so much from new things. Just to be present and let things happen.

Alex is going to go with me to the camp! She's not going to be a councilor though. Which is fine of course. I'm just glad I'm going to know someone there. It'll make it less scary to go to.

I'm really excited for a fresh start.

A new job.

That camp.

A chance to meet other kids and teens like me, but different. A chance to learn about other types of depressions and their depths. A chance to help other people be happy.

I'm happy. I really am. And I love the feeling of it! I think it suits me.

Yours Truly,

Abigail Mitchell

Seventeenth Entry:

Hi hi! Oh my gosh. I'm having such a great time at this camp! It's nothing like I expected. It's such an upbeat, fun and full of love place. To be honest I was thinking it'd be a lot gloomier. Having a whole bunch of people together, depressed or recovering… It sounds like a downer right? But it's not! Far from it actually!

The group I'm in charge of is all girls. There's five of us in our cabin and it's so much fun. The ages range from ten to fifteen. I wish Alex was in my group, but she's not. That's okay though! I still get to see her each day at the mess hall and when the groups meet up after dinner, every evening for a camp fire. It's great! We roast marshmallows and make s'mores!

You'll never guess what!

Dylan is here! He surprised me. He was on the sub sheet for councilors. He last minute subbed in for another councilor because she got sick and couldn't come. I know what you're thinking, Dylan isn't depressed. I know. But his sister Lexi has been coming to this camp for the past three summers and Dylan is great with her, so this is a perfect place for him. I definitely don't mind!

I fall for him more and more each day. I mean how can I not! He's so good with children. Dylan is in charge of an all guys group. There's four of them. Ages eight to eleven. His group is a lot younger than mine. Which is crazy to think… Kids that young can get depressed.

Three of them are orphan's and the fourth lives with his grandmother. But she's getting really old. I feel really bad for them all. But Dylan is doing an excellent job with them.

I honestly feel so terrible for all of these kids and teens. I'm so happy I decided to come to this camp. They might not see it yet, but I can see so much improvement in everyone. Just the simple fact of them smiling more often. And laughing. Some of these kids laughs are so beautiful and so contagious! You can tell it's been too long since they've really laughed. I'm happy to be a part of it now.

Next week the camp coordinates are bringing all of us on a field trip to an animal shelter. I'm so excited!!! Oh, and I'm excited for my group too! Spending time with animals is very helpful to people who suffer from depression. But it can also be very overwhelming for some. It will be a good learning experience for me and I hope my girls too.

I can't explain how good it feels to be here. I can really notice a difference in all the campers and I love it. I can see they are starting to get on the right track. And I hope they stay with it! All of these kids and teens are so beautiful and special in their own ways. You can't help but fall in love with them. I'm totally coming back here next summer, and the one after that and after that! As long as I can. I love this feeling. I love being able to help others. Especially youth.

I hope I'm making a difference in their lives, because they definitely have made a huge difference in mine!

Yours Truly,

Abigail Mitchell

Camp was so much fun! It honestly was the best two weeks ever. I helped so many people and without knowing it, they helped me too. I can't wait to go back there next year. I made so many friends there and learned about more depressions, and different depths of the different depressions. It was an eye opening experience and I loved every minute of it!

The last night there was really cool. We all sat at the bonfire, like always, but this night was special. After we finished making the s'mores, all the councilors got together. We handed out these small boxes. Everyone got one. The kids, the teens and the councilors. These boxes were for keepsake. To take home some part of this camp with them, as a reminder of your time here when we all go back home. In hopes to come back the following summer. Hoping to see friends return next year, and also to make new ones next year. Some kids had boxes from their previous summers. And the coolest thing is that even if you miss one summer you can still come back. And some of those kids were there two years ago, missed last year and were back for this summer.

Everything is so inclusive. I literally mean everything. It's so great. No one can feel lonely here. It's like almost impossible!

Anyway, back to the little keepsake boxes! So, if you're a returning camper you took out whatever was in your box and threw it into the bonfire. (This happened the first night of the camp) It was like a good luck charm to have fun for the next two weeks. Everyone, during the two week camp at some point picks something to put in their keepsake box. Whether it's a leaf, dirt, rock, shell, etc, you put it in your keepsake box to take home with you. Doesn't matter what it was, just as long as it meant something to you. A lot of the kids and teens said that those boxes help as motivation to get better and that, so they can come back the following summer. It's so great! It gives everyone something to look forward to.

I wish when I was as young as some of these kids, I knew about this camp! I wish I had the help when I was that young. But I got it, in good time. And it helped and still helps, even sometimes when I don't even realize it.

Dylan is so amazing.

Like so amazing, I don't even know how to begin to explain how or why. He's just the best.

I start school again in just over a week.

Senior Year.

Yikes!

I'm actually looking forward to it though. Dylan and I have some classes together. So that'll be great! I still have my part time job at the ice cream store, I'll just be working sometimes on weekends now that I'll be back at school! I'm looking forward to this year. I feel like I have a lot of good things coming my way.

Yours Truly,

Abigail Mitchell

Nineteenth Entry:

It's the night before my last first day of high school, and of course, I'm freaking out.

Dylan just left my house… We got into a fight. I think this was our first like real fight and I don't really remember half of it. I kind of blacked out. All I know is Dylan just left. Before he slammed my bedroom door shut he said he was tired of dealing with me. Then he slammed the door shut and took off.

I'm sitting on my floor and I don't know what to do. Alex is out of town until tomorrow and she doesn't have her phone with her, so I have no one to talk to. I'm just so angry at myself right now and I don't know what to do about it. And what's really pissing me off is that I don't remember what happened. I don't know why he left. It's honestly all blank, all black, nothing.

I don't think I've ever felt like this before. I never want to feel like it again.

All I want is to talk to Dylan right now. But I've never seen him so angry before, and I'm pretty sure he wouldn't pick up if I called him, anyway.

Ugh. I don't know what to do.

AND I have school tomorrow… I still don't know what I'm going to wear.

This is so stupid. What an awful day.

Why can't I remember what happened? This is actually starting to freak me out, like a lot. I've never blacked out before….

What happened?

I really hope Dylan is okay. I really do. I hope I didn't mess anything up… I mean I had such big plans for us in a few weeks. It'll be our anniversary and my dad is almost done burning off a CD I put together for him. It has all our favourite songs on it. We could sing them over and over again and never get tired of them.

Kind of like how I feel when I kiss Dylan or even look at him. No matter how many kisses or how many looks, it never gets old, and I love the feelings I get!

I really hope I didn't mess anything up.

This was going so good.

Why, why, why, do I always have to screw up everything when things are just getting good?

My first class tomorrow is Physics… With Dylan.

Wish me luck for that… I'm going to need it.

Yours Truly,

Abigail Mitchell

Twentieth Entry:

So… Today was kind of really weird.

I got to school and saw Dylan. He acted like nothing happened. I asked him if we could talk, and he said maybe later. He still kissed my forehead after walking me to my classes. We sat together at lunch. He drove me home after school. Normal. He couldn't come in because he had to pick his dad up from work to take him to pick up his car. Then they were going over to the hospital to visit with Lexi and their mom.

I honestly don't know what to do now…

I feel so lost. I hate feeling lost. I can't help but think about Alex right now, and how she blacks out sometimes from being so angry… Now me too?

What's happening to me?…

Well, um, I have a lot of homework. So I think I'm just going to go.

Wish me luck for tomorrow. Maybe Dylan will actually talk to me then…

Yours Truly,

Abigail Mitchell

Twenty First Entry:

Wow. Today was just... Where do I even begin...

Dylan and I talked. He told me that I freaked out on him, but that's it. He wouldn't tell me why. I kept asking him and all he would say is you figure it out... Well that's what I'm trying to do. I'm nervous and actually really concerned. I don't know what to think. I've never blacked out before. Why now? What triggered me to start now?

What if this wasn't the first time?

What if it's happened before but I never knew?

The razor blades...

I mean I've never thought of it before. Frankly, I tried to forget that even happened... But it does kind of make sense. Sleep walking isn't common in my family, or at least that we know of. I guess I never really put that much thought into how I got the razor blades, I just focused on the cuts.

Wow. What if...

I honestly don't know what to do. And no one was home yesterday when we fought so no one else heard us. I don't know if I should tell my parents or Alex or well, anyone. I think if I did it would make Dylan even more mad at me. I probably shouldn't... But I mean, I feel like someone else should know. Maybe they could look out for me. Watch for signs or possible triggers.

Another note, my parents are back to fighting. It was fine for a while. While I was doing better and when I came home from my camp it was great. But now it's back to the same old routine.

I feel like they should go see a councilor or get a divorce or something. Anything, really. Something needs to change, because this is just way too much. Like aren't they tired of fighting?

Remember that guy James? Um, he died today. Well last night I think. He tried another suicide attempt and this time it worked… His parents found him this morning on his floor in his room. They had to kick down the door because it was locked from the inside. There was a chair resting against the door to stop anyone from coming in. He left a note, saying he was sorry, but he couldn't handle life anymore.

I can't believe it. I just can't.

And this makes me even more scared, because what if I black out again and try again? I don't want to die, and I know that now, well I have for a while. I really am enjoying my life now. And I want to fix everything so it will all go back to normal.

I just want Dylan to talk to me and tell me what really happened… I want to fix things.

I think I love him, I want him to know that. But how can I tell him when he won't even speak to me now?

Yours Truly,

Abigail Mitchell

Twenty Second Entry:

I can't help but think that God has like forgotten about me or something. It's like once he helps make everything good he disappears and then I have no clue what to do and then it goes to shits again. I hate this pattern, things start to look like they'll be good, and they are for a little while. But as soon as I start to really get into the groove of things something changes and I'm back to square one.

I'm a mess.

I'm lost.

I'm a failure.

I'm never going to be good enough for anyone or anything.

UGH.

I just can't help but think lately that there's no hope for me. All I am is a big disappointment. A part of me kind of wants to try again. But this time I mean actually go through with it. But I don't know. I don't know if I'll be strong enough. Or weak enough. Or whatever you have to be to do it. I don't know how to do it. Not like I can ask anyone. I just don't know what to do. It's like everything around me is coming part, all at once, and I don't know how to stop or fix any of it. I'm trapped again. I'm trapped in my stupid thoughts again.

I hate this.

I hate my life.

I hate always messing up everything I ever do.

Maybe it wouldn't be such a bad thing if I did, yenno. I'd see James again.

This might be my last entry.

I'm sorry, but I can't anymore.

It's all too much.

It really is.

I just can't.

I'm sorry

Twenty Third Entry:

Hello journal, this is Abigail's Mother. I'm writing in here today to apologize for my lack of action. Abigail I am truly sorry. I never realized how much it meant to you, writing in this journal. Don't worry I won't read any of this, I just want to help you. Seeing that I have not done much, I am hoping this has.

Abigail you are unconscious right now, but you are doing just fine. All your vitals and levels are fine. It has been three days now and you have not regained consciousness yet. Though the doctors say you are doing good, I cannot help myself but worry. I want you to wake up soon baby girl. I want you to be happy again. Most of all I want you to know that you can trust me, that I'll always be there to listen to you and try to help in any way possible.

You know, I just heard about that boy James, who passed away. I work with his Mother. The whole family is broken right now, and all I can do is pray that you get better, Abigail. I really don't know what I would do if I lost my little Abi-bear. I know you said you have out grown that name, but it is still one of my favorites.

I understand now, how you did not like journaling at the beginning. I do not even know what to write or talk about now. Though I am really glad you have kept up with it. I hope one day you will share it with me or others, or not. It really does not matter. As long as my little girl continues to be happy, then I am happy. I really want to help you. I cannot help but think this is all my fault. I know you hear your Father and I fighting. I really am sorry about that. I do not want you to think it has anything to do with you. It's not. It's between just your Father and I. It's complicated. Marriage is not easy.

Anyway, I'm going to put your laptop away now. Maybe I'll read to you for a bit. The doctor said even though you cannot respond, you could still be listening. I hope you're listening Abigail. And I hope you wake up to read this, and continue to write in this journal. If I cannot help you I hope this does. And I will be right here holding your hand, doing my very best to be there for you. I am sorry for all the lost time. I know I will never be able to make it up to you, but I am willing to try.

Sincerely,

M. Mitchell

Twenty Fourth Entry:

Hi Journal, it's Alex and Abi! The doctors want Abi to rest, but she still wants to keep up with her journal, so here I am to help! She's finally awake! We're all so happy! I've been here every day, by Abi's side just waiting for her to wake up. She's doing great! Well as great as she can be under the circumstances. Oh yeah! You don't know yet, Abi said. Well, I'll tell you what happened! Well, Abi will tell me what to type, duh. Okay! Here goes!

Abi had another black out. She got a knife from her kitchen and took it upstairs to her bathroom and locked the door. She doesn't remember doing it at all. All she remembers is going to bed that night and now waking up in the hospital, 4 days later. She had cut her wrists, thighs and her stomach. She lost a lot of blood… Her mother is the one that found her. She was going to the bathroom in the middle of the night, around 3 am, and she saw a red stain coming through the bathroom door, and the light was on. She tried to open the door but it was locked from the inside. She shouted for Abi's Dad, and he came out with a key from their room. They unlocked the door and there she was. Abi was unconscious laying on the bathroom floor, in her own pool of blood. (Scary, right?) They called 911, and it's a good thing they found her when they did. The doctors said that if they found her just an hour or so later, they might not of been able to save her. They stabilized her and she stayed unconscious for 4 days. She's finally awake now. She still doesn't remember anything that happened. Dylan is here too. He's been great through this all. Both of us are so happy Abi will be okay.

Abi is going to have another nap now, so Dylan and I are going to pick up her homework from school and come back. I just want to leave you a little note Abi:

Girl, you are my inspiration. You might never understand why, or how. But you are. You're so strong and incredible. You may not feel like that right now, but I hope one day you will realize it. And when that day comes I'll be here! I'm so happy to have a friend like you. You are one heck of a gal, Abi! I honestly don't know where I would be today without you. And I hope you never forget that. You inspire people. You really do. I still get mail from all the campers, asking about you and hoping that you pull through, and I told them I knew you would. And you did! I called it! Well how could I not, when I already know the strength that's inside you. I know that you will get through this, and you will be out of the hospital soon! Because girl, they have amazing sales right now at the mall and how could I go with anyone but you! I need my Abi-girl to tell me how cute I look in everything, or how ugly! LOL! You always give your honest opinions, and girl do I ever miss them! Feel better soon baby girl!

P.s, Always remember I'm here for you, unconditionally. And I really do mean that. One hundred percent! You're like the sister I never had, but will forever keep! Love you to the moon and back.

Your Best Friend,

Alexandria Thorbune

Oh! I should sign as you, keep the tradition going! I hope you can write your own entry next, and if not I'll be here to help again! Love ya, girl.

Yours Truly,

Abigail Mitchell

Twenty Fifth Entry:

Hi, it's me. I'm finally back! I'm home now.

Wow.

I don't even know where to begin…

It's crazy how supportive everyone has been. My parents, my siblings, Alex, Dylan, Lexi, even some people from my school have sent me get well soon cards. I just wish I knew how to thank them. Really. I don't know how to deal with all this attention. But the good thing is, that it's all good attention. And I know that now. No one is here just to find out my secrets to tell their friends, the ones who are around are the ones who actually care and want to help me get better.

I just hope I don't disappoint them.

I still don't remember much.

I remember writing that entry, then I just went to bed… Next thing I know I wake up in a hospital room. I saw my mom and dad, and I saw Alex and Dylan. They were all just sitting there, patiently waiting.

Four days.

Four days I was out.

Four days of my life I will never get back.

Four days of their lives they will never get back.

How?!

And the weirdest things are happening too. I can't help but think there's stuff that they aren't telling me. Something happened while I was unconscious and I want to find out what. I don't care how big or small it is, I want to know. I don't want to be out of the loop. They can trust me. They should know that.

Dylan came by earlier today, before he had to go to school. He apologized for storming out of the house that night. And I forgave him. And he forgave me. He doesn't really remember what the fight was about, and that's okay with me I guess. As long as we can move past it and be okay. I just want things to go back to the way they used to be. Happy.

Dylan made me cry today...

Happy tears!

He looked at me and said, "Baby, I'm not going anywhere. I need you in my life, just as much as you need me. I'm here for you, unconditionally. I hope you never forget that. Yes we may fight, but all couples do, that's normal. It'd be weird if we didn't. I'm going to look out for you, because I care about you. I love you"

"I love you, too."

Yours Truly,

Abigail Mitchell

Twenty Sixth Entry:

Hi.

Okay so I don't know what to do about my family… They're acting so strange and it's like totally obvious. Something happened, and I just want to know what. I'm a big girl, I can handle it. Yes, I know I shouldn't be doing anything to add unnecessary stress on me, but I can't help but stress out not knowing. Soo, wouldn't it just be better if they told me? I mean, come on whatever it is can't be that bad.

Right…?

On another note, Dylan is so amazing!

Well I know you already knew that, but I don't care. I could keep saying it over and over again and never get tired of it! I mean, like seriously. Over and over and over again. He's like perfect, so perfect…

Did I mention he's kind of perfect? Well, ya. He is!

Dylan gave me a promise ring. It's gorgeous. He gave it to me after he said he loves me. It was such a perfect night. He said he was planning it for a while, and wanted to make it just perfect. And oh boy, it was perfect. He makes me so happy. He makes me look forward to my future. He makes me a better me.

I just wish my family was as honest as Dylan is.

They need to know they can trust me. I mean, I trust them. Why can't they trust me back? It's not like I have a ton of friends to go and gossip to or whatever. It's not like I'm going to stop loving them or something stupid like that. We're family. We're stuck together for life.

So why, why, why are they not being honest with me?????????????

I honestly don't know how many times I've asked.

I've been home now for a couple days. I'm doing fine, health wise. I'm on schedule. I'm recovering.

What else do I have to do?

I just want some answers.

Oh! I've got other news.

I'm going to see a different therapist tomorrow. Alex has gone to this one before. Apparently he is super nice and actually cares about you. Alex said he's like a funny Uncle dude. (She has a funny way of describing people). Anyway, this therapist is going to help me remember my blackouts. Well at least try to. I don't really know how it works. There's a chance it won't even work, but I mean what's the worst thing that could happen? I don't remember the night that I already don't remember? It's worth a shot. Wish me luck!

Yours Truly,

Abigail Mitchell

Twenty Seventh Entry:

Hi… It didn't work.

Well, I'm not that surprised. BUT it rarely works the first try anyway. So I'm going back in a couple days to try again. It was really cool though. Like the process. I've never done anything like it before. I had to lay down on this couch, eyes closed and keep my body still. Then the guy talked me through different scenarios and I'd talk back to him. Telling him things I saw or smelt or felt or anything really. We started with big events that I could tell you right off the top of my head. Easy things to start. Then once I was comfortable he changed it to that night. But it was black. All black. Nothing.

Strange right?

I don't understand how someone can just forget something that they did. Especially cutting themselves… And then waking up four days later in a hospital bed.

I'm actually really good at remembering things. I have a great memory. Well, I've always hated it because I rarely forget things, so when I get really depressed it's not that hard to think of even more things to add to my already horrible moods. But now I'm blank. There's nothing up there from that night. It just doesn't make any sense to me. Like at all. I just don't understand.

I'm going to an EA meeting tomorrow. My first meeting back. It's the Wednesday group so I don't know them as well as the Saturday group, so I hope they won't judge me. Well I know they're not supposed to, It's inclusive. It's a beautiful place actually. And I'm actually excited to be going back. I need that group. Maybe they need me too. A lot of them inspire me, maybe I'll end up helping one of them.

Ah, I miss helping people.

I don't know what any of the campers would say or do if they knew about this. I think Alex mentioned that she spoke to a few of them while I was out, but she didn't really say anything specific. Come to think of it no one has said anything really specific about anything since I woke up.

Dylan has been the only honest one with me.

I did ask him if he knew what had happened but he said he wasn't sure. He said that they didn't tell him anything, and he thought they were just acting weird because they were afraid of something else happening to me. I mean, I don't blame them. Knowing my mother she probably thought of the worst possible outcomes of me being unconscious and then told everyone.

I just can't help but think they're hiding something. They are acting weird and I know it's something more than just being worried something worse was going to happen to me.

I just know it. I have a strong feeling, you know? A gut feeling. It's something.

I just wish they'd tell me already. UGH. Wish me luck…

Yours Truly,

Abigail Mitchell

Twenty Eighth Entry:

Hi, I'm just having a snack then going to the meeting. Alex should be here soon. We're going together.

I'm kind of nervous… I don't know why…

Well I just wanted to do a quick check in before I go.

My day was interesting. My dad stayed home with me today. He got the day off work. He made me food and we watched a movie… And that's it. He barely spoke to me. It's like he didn't know how to talk to me… I guess I can't really blame him. He doesn't understand. Frankly, I don't even understand it either…

Well, I better go. I'll write when I get back from the meeting.

Wish me luck.

***

I'm back.

Wow… Remember how I said I thought everyone was hiding something from me… Well, it's true. They were. I don't even know where to begin. It's not even one thing… I just can't actually believe this right now. I don't know if I should be happy or if I should be sad or if I should be angry… I thought I was a mess before. My incident seems like nothing now…

Ok… well… um…

Remember how I told you that Dylan's mom was sick. She has cancer. Well, um, had it. She passed away.

Day 2 of being unconscious.

She's gone…

It all happened so fast.

And that's not all… Lexi (you know Dylan's little sister) well she has cancer now too. She was diagnosed the day before her mother passed away.

AND my sister is pregnant.

I don't even know what to do now. I want to be happy for my sister yes, but how can I be happy when Mrs. Michaels is dead, and now little Lexi has cancer.

I thought my life was a mess before. Well, frankly, I thought it was fine then I cut myself and went for a four day nap and woke up and realized I wasn't fine, then I think I'm fine and now everything is not fine, but I just wish it was fine because this time last year everything seemed to be fine, but a year later my whole life is falling apart and I'm only 17 years old.

Hi my name is Abigail Melanie Mitchell, I am 17 years old and I am a complete mess.

BUT WAIT THERE IS MORE.

My parents filed for divorce.

Wonderful.

Fantastic.

Just great.

The icing on top of this piece of shit cake of a life.

I honestly have no clue what to do with myself right now. I thought talking about all of this would make me feel better, but honestly it's just making me feel worse. I'm realizing just how serious it all is. And then it makes me want to talk even more. But how do I even talk about these things without stressing myself out, but trying to figure this out is stressing me out and I'm not actually doing anything I'm just rambling and don't know how to stop myself.

I'm a mess.

But I can't be a mess.

Dylan.

He needs me.

I can't help but think he only told me he loved me and gave me that ring because of the circumstances. But then I know him and even if things were okay after I woke up he still would of done it. I know his feelings are true. But how could he not tell me. He seemed to be the only person being honest with me. But he kept the biggest lies.

I guess I can't really blame him. I mean he's a bigger mess than me right now. I don't know how he even had the energy to wait around for me to wake up. Or how he has spent all the time he has with me. How is he not with his family right now.

I guess he's just lost. I mean, I would be too. Yeah, I don't get along great with my parents but I don't know what I would do if anything bad ever happened to them. And Dylan was so close to his mother.

I don't know how he's being so strong right now. I guess Lexi chose a lion as her favourite animal because Dylan is literally the human version of a lion.

Oh no. Lexi.

Little Lexi…

Okay God, I know you have a path for everyone and everything happens for a reason. Yes I believe in you. But I'm sorry, I can't help but question you right now as to… Why? Why? Why? WHY?!

Yours Truly,

Abigail Mitchell

Sorry it's been a few days since I've last written in here.

The funeral for Mrs. Michaels was today. It was a beautiful service. She was a beautiful woman, and she'll never be forgotten. Ever. She was so strong even in her final days. Mr. Michaels told me that even on her last day she was still asking about me, praying for me, praying I would wake up and be okay and she was the one who had it worse off than me. She was an angel, and now she's our guardian angel.

Omg, I just feel so horrible for that family.

Lexi has the exact same leukemia. It's probably going to be even worse for her because she's so young. She's just so small. I have no clue how her little body is going to be able to handle all that chemotherapy. I know she's tough and she's a fighter, but I don't know if that's enough…

On another note, my sister is doing well. Her and her fiancé are moving back into our house. Just so they can be closer to mom and dad, and it'll be easier to raise a baby here than in a small little apartment in NYC.

Mom and Dad are still getting a divorce though.

I don't know how this is going to work.

I'm hoping that by my sis moving back home, maybe they'll come to some kind of agreement and all of us could try to be a family again.

I know I'd really like that.

I also feel really bad for Dylan.

I think it just finally sunk in that his mother is gone, today. He probably was trying not to think about it and hoped it was all a lie and he'd just wake up and everything would go back to the way things were just a week ago.

Wow.

It's crazy how so many things can happen in such a short period of time. I mean really. Like so much has happened in just a week...

I can't really wrap my head around any of it.

I'm going to that therapist again tomorrow. I had to post pone the meeting because of the funeral and all that, so tomorrow I'm finally going. And now I'm super nervous about it. I already have so much on my plate right now, I'm kind of not sure if I can handle, yenno... remembering.

Well, wish me luck for tomorrow. I'm going to need it.

Yours Truly,

Abigail Mitchell

Thirtieth Entry:

Okay so if I didn't know what to do before, now it's official.

Dylan is such a mess and my heart is aching just looking at him. He's staying the night at my house tonight. He's passed out in my chair and he looks so cute sleeping but I know he's not having a good rest. Tossing and turning. He's exhausted. I know it. I don't blame him either. His mom is gone. It's still hard for me to believe it. I can't imagine how he feels right now. I want to ask him, but I'm afraid to upset him even more. But what if he wants to talk about it? But if he wanted to talk about it he would of done so already, right? Maybe he's just scared.

I brought up the idea of journaling to him the other day. He kind of just brushed it off. But today he brought it up. He said he might look into it. I hope he does. I think it'd be good for him. I know how hard it is to talk sometimes and having a journal with no judgment is a great way to sort things out. I hope he at least tries it. I know he's done it before with Lexi but they both kind of just grew away from it. I don't really know if he liked it or not. I'm just hoping he does now. If he's too afraid to talk to me, then I'd much rather him write in a journal. Anything really. So that he doesn't keep everything all bottled up inside. That's not healthy. So if it's not me, I'd be comfortable knowing he can tell his journal. Then just sit back and wait. Hope that maybe he'll want to share it with me as well. And if not, that's totally cool with me.

I love him. I want what's best for him.

I just wish there was more for me to do. I feel lost not being able to do much. Yes, he keeps saying how grateful he is to have me around but I feel like I could be helping him so much more. But I'm lost too. I mean like I lost four days of my life. I thought I was fine… Well turns out I'm not. I missed so much. I can't believe Mrs. Michaels is gone. I really, really, really wish I was there for Dylan when it happened. That's probably what I feel worst about. I'm his girlfriend. We're like best friends. And I wasn't there for him when he needed me most. I guess it's still great I'm here now, and believe me I'm not going anywhere. I just feel like there's so much lost time we'll never get back.

Both of our lives are constantly changing and I feel like we're each other's safe zones. It's like no matter how shitty our days were, when we're together things brighten up a bit. It's just comforting knowing he is my constant.

I don't know what I would do if anything happened to him. I don't even know what to do now that everyone in his family is getting sick. I feel awful. I feel like a bad girlfriend. But I'm honestly doing the best I can right now. I'm just being there for him. I'm holding space. I'm there for him but I'm giving him his space he needs. I know he'll come to me eventually. He always does.

I think that's why he's spending so much time with me. Everyone grieves differently. When he's home all his dad does is ask him questions. His heart is in the right space yes, but that's just not how Dylan likes to deal with things. He needs his time. And I respect that.

I just hope he knows he can trust me with anything. I'm always going to be here for him. Always.

Yours Truly,

Abigail Mitchell

Thirty First Entry:

Okay I'm sorry but this therapy thing is a joke. I've gone three times now and nothing. Big fat nothing. I feel like I'm just wasting the guys time and mine. I'm so anal about time lately. Can't blame me right. I mean I lost four days of my life. Four days I'll never get back. Yeah, I know I've already said that but I can't help it. Like sometimes I just feel like such a failure.

I should be enjoying my senior year of high school with my super hot boyfriend. I should be going to parties and getting stupid drunk with friends. I should be planning what color prom dress I want. I should be doing normal teenage girl stuff.

But no.

Nope.

Instead, I'm being home schooled. I go to the hospital daily. If it isn't for a checkup for me, it's to go see Lexi. I have to take breaks after doing things for too long of a period of time. For example, if I take more than an hour to write this entry I'm going to have to stop. Get up. Go for a walk around my house. Get a snack or some kind of tea or water. Then sit back down ten-ish minutes later just to finish this. It's crazy. It's stupid. But apparently it's necessary. I'm 17 years old and I can't live a normal life. Frankly, I've never been 'normal' but even if I wanted to be there's no going that way now. Not when I have to be monitored daily. My parents think they're being sly. But they're not. They've even got my sister into doing it now. Yeah you guessed it, she's all moved in. Her fiancé still works so it's just us two at home. And when my home school teacher comes over, my sister takes a nap. But before my teacher leaves I have to wake her up so she can say good-bye. I can't remember the last time I was alone for more than a two minute pee.

Oh my gosh.

I can't even shower alone. My sister will make up some lame excuse like she has to pluck her eye brows and the main bathroom has the best lighting, and seeing that I'm going to be showering she can do her eye brows at the same time so she doesn't get bored and has someone to talk to.

And get this.

If I want to shave my legs I have to get either my mom or sister to help me. They don't trust me to do it by myself. They don't trust me to be alone. Okay I understand that they don't want anything to happen to me again. Yes, I understand that. But come on. I think they're going just a little too much over board with all this stuff? Like come on I'm fine. I'm doing very well. I just wish they'd let me live my life.

If they want me to get better. If they want me to recover and eventually live a 'normal' life, they're going to have to let me live and make my own mistakes and stop treating me like a child. Okay yes I understand their concern. But this is just too much.

It's almost been an hour so I should go before my sister gets mad. Wish me luck.

Yours Truly,

Abigail Mitchell

Thirty Second Entry:

Hey, it's Dylan.

Abi wants me to try journaling but I don't know.

It seems kind of stupid.

It helps her I know but I don't think it will help me.

I um don't really know what to say.

I miss my mom.

Lexi is doing fine.

The chemotherapy seems to be working.

She lost her hair though.

I went pretty fast.

But she's a trouper.

She gets it from me.

I kind of wish it was me that got sick not Lexi. She doesn't deserve it.

Well no one deserves it.

But if it could be anyone, I wish it was me not her.

I love my sister. I hate seeing her like this.

Um that's all I got.

See ya later, probably.

Abi is probably going to make me make my own journal.

I guess that'd be okay. I'll try it.

For her.

-Dylan Michaels

Thirty Third Entry:

Hi hi! I don't really have a lot of time right now to talk, but I wanted to do a quick check in anyways.

I met with one of my campers today.

Meghan!

Alex told her what happened to me and she wanted to come and see me as soon as I got better. And I've been home for a while now so we made plans for lunch!

Of course my sister had to go with me… But it was alright because she sat at a different table in the food court so I had at least some privacy with Meghan.

Meghan is doing great! I'm so happy to hear about her. She's been volunteering at her local animal shelter. Remember how I told you that working with animals can really be beneficial to depressed people? Well it's true and it works for her! She goes there two days a week after school, and all day Saturdays! She told me if I ever wanted to come and visit with the animals to call and she'll book me in no problem!

She's such a sweet, genuine and fabulous girl. She's going to go far in life, I just know it.

She has so much drive and motivation.

It's hard to believe that she used to be depressed.

It still amazes me how normal all the depressed people I meet look. But once other people find out they are depressed they treat them differently and they become outcasts.

Honestly though I think all these depressed people are such beautiful human beings. It takes strength and courage to live your life to the fullest you can when your 'normal', and it's extraordinary to see someone who's depressed show up to school or EA meetings smiling and happy. Even if it's just an act, it takes guts to even get out of bed. I applaud them all for it.

I've got to go though. I'm going to see a movie with my sister.

Don't worry it's rated G so I'm okay to see it. It won't stress me out or anything.

And believe me it took a lot of convincing to get my sister to take me.

I just need to get out of this house!

I'll talk to you tomorrow!

Yours Truly,

Abigail Mitchell

Wow. Hi.

I just got back from the hospital.

Lexi has no hair now… It's crazy. I just saw her like two days ago and she still had her full head of hair… And no she has none.

My mom and I are bringing over some cute fun wigs tomorrow to surprise her. I hope she'll like them. I just want her to be happy. Even though she's going through all this chemo she still deserves to smile. And I want to help as much as possible.

We're so close. She's like the little sister I never had. I actually love my relationship with Lexi.

Dylan says he falls for me even more when he watches me with Lexi. Dylan said, "It's like you two have been sisters for your whole lives, even though you just met almost one year ago."

I love the Michaels family so much.

It's really difficult not having Mrs. Michaels around anymore. Believe it or not but their family is closer than ever. I appreciate that. And now I'm really a part of it. I still wish Mrs. Michaels was here. Especially for Lexi. She needs her mother right now, and that's something I can't do for her and it breaks my heart. Though my mom has been spending a lot of time at the hospital with me and with Lexi. So Lexi has my mom and I. I know it's not the same. But it's better than nothing, right?

I'm going to see that therapist tomorrow.

I told my parents I'd go tomorrow, but it'd be the last time. I just feel like it's a waste of time. It's not going to work. I'm not going to remember. So there's no point in wasting any more time on it.

I do want to remember, but I just think I'm not ready yet.

I want to find out eventually, but not right now and that's okay with me. I just hope that my parents will finally understand that too. It's too much for me right now. I'll go back when I'm ready. To be honest, I don't really know when I'll be ready or if I'll ever be ready. All I know is I need more time. I'm just getting back to a normal routine and all that. I need more consistency in my life for now. I need more balance. Once I get that, then maybe I'll go back and try again. I just think it makes sense, you know? If my brain is all over the place right now, and stressed out about other stuff and people, it's going to be more difficult to remember anything. But if I get into a good vibe, and I'm happy and I don't really have a lot on my plate anymore, then I think I could go the distance. I could really dive into the therapy, and try to remember. Like I said, I do want to remember. When I'm ready.

So wish me luck for tomorrow!

Yours Truly,

Abigail Mitchell

Thirty Fifth Entry:

My sister just woke me up.

I remember…

***

Hey it's Abigail's sister. I'm writing in here because I just found Abigail talking in her sleep. I was told to write down anything out of the ordinary that she does. I was walking past her room and heard her talking and I thought she was still up, maybe on the phone with someone. I wanted to check in on her of course. But when I looked in her room she was fast asleep. She was shaking physically and speaking very weird. I didn't really know what to do and I saw her laptop open on her desk so I figured I should maybe listen for a while and write down things she says. I'll show her in the morning too, see if she remembers any of it. Abigail keeps saying James' name. I'm pretty sure it's the guy from her school who killed himself. I think that was his name. She's mumbling a lot. Hard to kind of make out what she's saying. She keeps shaking. I don't know if I should wake her or not. She's talking now with a weird voice. It's like she's trying to talk like a guy. I don't like the sounds or looks of this. I'm going to wake her up. I'll see if she'll talk to me. Or at least write all this down.

The Night

Rolling around in her bed. Abigail is unable to sleep. Tossing and turning she sees a figure in the corner of her room. Rubbing her eyes, it becomes clear it's a person. With a closer look she sees her friend James.

"James, is that you?" she asks.

"Yes."

Abigail says confused, "But I don't understand. You're dead."

After a long period of silence, James replies, "Abigail. I am here. I am here in your room with you. I see you and you see me. Right? Right. I need someone to talk to. I need someone to help me. I need your help. I want to cross over. I want to be free. I need your help. I need guidance. Abigail will you help me?"

Shocked, Abigail doesn't know how to reply or what to do. Suddenly Abigail feels trapped in her bed. She can't get up. She can't move. She's stuck, almost trapped. She finally says, "Um, yeah sure. I can try. What happened to you? What drove you that far? Your life seemed fine. Why did you do it James?"

"No one cared about me. Sure I had a lot of friends but they were just friends. None of them were close to me. Once school was over for the day it's like I didn't exist anymore. They all would go hang out together and never invite me. Ever. They would say things like they had tons of homework to do so they would just see me tomorrow at school. But later that night I would see them posting things on Facebook or Twitter. I knew they were hanging out, they just didn't want me around. Then I would question them the next day at school. They would always make up some excuse like how one of them came over to study then they finished and decided randomly to go see a movie or something like that. It was all bullshit. My whole life was a joke. I was this star athlete, sure. But that was it. I was everyone's friend on the field but once the games and practices were over, so was I."

"James, I'm so sorry. I had no idea."

Totally ignoring Abigail's comment, James continues, "It all adds up. The broken promises. The lies. Everything. I started cutting my thighs to feel something other than numbness."

Abigail mumbles, "Me too."

Unaware, again, James continues, "Then one day after a tough football game. I was in the locker room after everyone left and I attempted to hang myself. Before I could go through with it my coach found me. He stopped me. He got me help. He also kept it quiet so no one else would know. I didn't want them to have any more excuses not to hang out with me. He got me the help, sure but it was useless. I felt like the therapist didn't care at all about me. It's like he had anything and everything else on his mind but helping me. My parents didn't know about it. No one did. Just my coach, the therapist and me. I couldn't tell anyone. I was embarrassed. I felt like an idiot. But they drove me that way. It's their fault. No one showed interest in me. Or my feelings. Or anything about me."

"Wow, I wonder if our therapists are related." Abigail jokes. Trying to lighten the mood a little.

Still oblivious, James continues, "We kept it a secret for a while. But then I just stopped going. I also stopped going to practices. It all was just becoming too much for me to handle. I started cutting myself more regularly. It was the only thing that made me actually feel something. I was in control of something in my life. Control. I finally had control." Silence hit the room. After a few moments James picks back up. "Then I lost it. I lost everything. But I was okay with it. I thought who cares? Literally no one. One night I decided I had enough. I locked my door. Put a chair up against it. Waited until everyone was sleeping. I cut my thighs, my stomach, my wrists, my forearms. I laid there on my floor and I was happy. I was happy because I knew it was the end of my misery."

With tears rolling down her face, sniffling Abigail tried to answer, "James, you had me."

"What?"

"James, you always had someone. You always had me. Don't you remember? In grade three we promised to always be friends no matter what. We promised to always have each other's backs. Don't you remember that?" Abigail asks.

"Abs I honestly don't…"

There's a moment of connection. Abigail tries to get up to hug him. She's still trapped. She finally says, "James, why are you here? I don't understand."

"I need you Abigail. Come with me. Come through the light with me. We could make up for lost time. We could be best friends again. We could be together until the end of time. Abigail come with me. Abigail I need you." James hands her a knife from her kitchen.

Hesitant Abigail doesn't know what to do. All of a sudden she in her bathroom. Questioning what is going on Abigail realizes the door is locked. She's trapped again. She thinks about her friend James. Wondering if that was real. She hears a voice in the back of her head, "Abigail I need you. Abigail you need me. Abigail… Abi… Abs…"

Now in tears Abigail doesn't know what to do. She cries. She's powerless. She feels weak. She feels numb. She knows what it's like not to be numb. She has a choice to make.

Four Days Later

Abigail wakes up in a hospital bed. Not knowing where she is. She is in a pale blue hospital gown. She is hooked up to an IV. Suddenly she feels pain from her thighs, stomach and left wrist. She realizes what she's done. She finally notices her family surrounding her. Abigail finally speaks.

"How long have I been her for?"

"Four days sweetheart." Her father replies. "We were worried about you."

"Four days?" Asked Abigail. "What do you mean four days? I was just in my room…"

"It's okay sweetheart, it's been a rough few days. Try and get some rest. We can talk in the morning."

And like that Abigail was alone, again. Her family left the room one by one, after giving her hugs and forehead kisses goodnight. Abigail was trapped… Again. Waking up hooked to an IV, dressed in a hospital gown, nothing was familiar to her at all. And then she heard a voice. Looking at her window she saw her friend James. This time he was a ghost like figure. He still looked like himself, but see-through. Abigail was speechless.

"Thank you," he whispered.

A light brighter than the sun shone through the window, and Abigail watched as her third grade best friend disappeared into the light. And then the light was gone. Abigail was left in her bed, again, alone. Confused and exhausted, Abigail fell asleep.

Abigail awoke the next morning to a nurse bringing in some breakfast for her. It looked amazing, and tasted even better. The first meal

Abigail ate in over four days. Not long after her parents arrived with a bag of clothing. Abigail was being released later that evening after they ran a few more tests.

Thirty Fifth Entry Continued:

Wow.

Hi.

If I wasn't confused before I sure am now…

Did I actually see James? Did he actually give me the kitchen knife? Did he actually pass on? Was that really his ghost? But if I saw him in what looked like real life form in my room, and ghost like in my hospital room… No. It couldn't of been him? Could it? I mean he did look pretty real to me…

But no!

Come on. My sister just woke me up, it must of just been a dream.

But how was it so real in my head.

I mean it does match up to everything… At least I think it does.

I just can't get over James… Did I really help him pass on to a better place? Or was I dreaming it? Was he waiting for me to actually join him…?

I don't know what to say or do right now. Like do I tell somebody or do I keep this to myself.

James' parents would want to know that he's moved on to better.

No, Abigail. It was just a dream…

…ok but what if it wasn't… They would want to know… Wouldn't they?

No.

Maybe that'll just make things worse.

Oh my gosh.

I can't handle this.

I'm making a tea then going back to bed.

I'll figure this out in the morning.

Wish me luck.

Yours Truly,

Abigail Mitchell

Thirty Sixth Entry:

Good morning. Okay so I called James' parents… I had to.

I'm going to have lunch with them later today. They were really happy to hear from me, they said they often asked James about me and it was a shame that we had drifted apart in high school.

Wow…

I don't know what to do or say now… I mean like I'm going to go see them either way.

But do I tell them? Or do I not?

I don't know how they're going to react to me if I say anything, especially if I say it was what I thought was just a dream.

I mean that's all it was right? A dream…. But, then why did it feel so real?

I can't bare the thought of hurting them even more… I mean come on they just lost their only son. I know how close they all were. Maybe it'd be better if I didn't say anything. Maybe it'd be better for them just to see me. A familiar face. Catch up from when I last saw them.

Ugh, I don't know what I'm going to do.

I guess I'll figure it out when I get there.

Wish me luck!! I'm seriously going to need it!

***

Whoa, that was an interesting lunch..

James' parents looked surprisingly good, I mean in spite of the circumstances.

We ate and talked about school, casual things. They got a dog a couple years ago that I didn't even know about. They showed me pictures, it's so cute! A chocolate lab, my favourite!

After we finished eating his dad looked at me and said that they know James is in a better place now… I was shocked, I didn't know how to react.

He continued on to tell me that he knew he wasn't doing well and it was heartbreaking to know that, but in the end they both were glad he wasn't suffering anymore. They wished they'd of known sooner, because maybe they would have been able to help him. But they seem to be okay with it.

I decided to tell them… I explained that I thought it was just a dream, and the weirdest thing happened… While I was telling them, well, I couldn't really make eye contact with them so I was playing with my water glass, and when I finally finished and looked up at the two of them, they had tears in their eyes… But they had the biggest smiles on their faces. The same big smiles I remember from when I was little.

"You were his 'unfinished business', Abi," James' mom said to me… Me? Why me?...

Yours Truly,

Abigail Mitchell

It took me forever to figure out what James' mom meant… I think I get it now. I mean like I think it makes sense. I could of been his unfinished business. He knew I was depressed, he know I was picked on in school and he knew I would understand. And he remembered how close we used to be, so I'm guessing he figured we have a new commonality that maybe I would join him. And I guess I tried to join him, though I woke up… He still thanked me. Maybe that's all he needed, To know I'd still do anything for him. And this just wasn't my time to join him.

I will one day. But not yet. Definitely not yet.

I've got a lot of living left to do.

You know, in a way, I kind of want to dedicate a part of my life to him. All the fun I'll have doing things will be extra fun because of him. Because he was my best friend and he always will be. People drift apart. So what. It's the true ones that come back right? And he came back to me. I think I owe him that much. And that way, when my time comes, and I finally am with him again I'll have a ton of awesome stories to tell him.

Wow, it's crazy how much you can miss someone that you used to be so close to so long ago. A part of me is kind of bummed out that we drifted apart. I don't even know how it happened. I know he kind of got popular and that but why did he have to stop talking to me? Huh, well I guess I'll never know. I can't help but wonder what kind of a man he would of turned out to be if he just gave himself one more year.

Someone told me once that if something big and serious is on your mind don't act on it right away. Wait, and if it's still lingering around six months to a year later then revisit it. Possibly act on it or do something to change it...

I wish I could of told James that... If he just waited one more year. We would have been graduated high school. He wouldn't of had to see anyone we went to school with anymore. Maybe he would of gotten a scholarship to a university out of town... He had such a bright future ahead of him.

We all do really.

You know what, I have a bright future ahead of me, and no one can take that from me. I won't let them. Just look at what I've overcome! I'm a trooper for goodness sakes!

Speaking of troopers, you should see Little Lexi. She's doing amazing with her chemo. She's definitely a trooper. Just like her mom. I know she's going to win this battle. She has to..

I can't lose anyone else. I don't think I have that in me.

I'm at a good place in my life right now. Well considering everything. But I'm managing and that's what counts. I don't feel lost anymore to be honest. I finally feel like I'm figuring out just who I want to be.

Dylan is taking me out for dinner tonight. So I'm going to go get ready.

Like always, wish me luck!

Yours Truly,

Abigail Mitchell

Thirty Eighth Entry:

Hi hi hi!

Okay remember last summer when I went to that camp?! Well I just got an email from the president of the camp and they want me to come back this summer! AH! I'm so excited right now. Honestly that was such an amazing experience and to be asked to come back is a honor!

I hadn't even thought that far ahead yet! I mean you can't really blame me. But I will for sure be there again this summer. No matter what.

Those campers made such a huge impact on my life, there is no way I'd miss it. I really hope I've affected them even half the amount they've affected me. Just knowing I've helped a few people even just get out of bed in the morning and show up to the mess hall for breakfast or to an arts and crafts session, really means the world to me.

I know for a fact some people don't realize and probably never will, just how hard simple day-to-day tasks are for some people. Making meals, doing laundry, heck even just getting out of bed in the morning and showing up for the day can be difficult. Believe me, I know.

Speaking of the campers, I was talking to that girl Meghan that works at the animal shelter the other day. I'm going to take Lexi out Saturday for the afternoon and we're going to visit her! It'll be great to see Meghan again, see how she's been doing. Also, it'll be a fun day for Lexi. She hasn't left her hospital room in so long. She could be going to different activity groups on her floor of the hospital, but she doesn't want to. I'm a little concerned for her. But I'm not over stepping, because she's been through a lot. I just want to be there for her whenever she decides she wants to talk, or if she doesn't want to talk then I'll be there just to be there. She's the little sister I never had. That's why I'm taking her to the shelter Saturday. I think it'll be good for the both of us.

Another note!

I'm going to be able to go to my high school prom!!! Yay!

Dylan was buying a ticket for the dinner portion and the girl at the desk asked if I would be joining him. Dylan was shocked. He hadn't put much thought into it. Can't blame him. His mind is still all over the place. The girl said that I was missed at school and it'd be a great way for me to catch up with everyone.

I was shocked.

I'm missed at school? People actually miss me? Me? Abigail? Like me? Abi the freak?

Wow. Well I guess people can surprise you.

I'm just happy to be able to go dress shopping!! Oh my gosh! I don't even know what color dress I'd want to get. Should I wear heels or flats or cute strappy sandals?! Or do I wait and pick out my shoes after I have my dress. Yeah. That sounds right. But what if I find the perfect shoes and they don't go with the dress I picked out. Then what do I do. Oh. My. God. I don't even know where to begin!!

I'm going to go talk to my sister. Wish me luck!

Yours Truly,

Abigail Mitchell

Thirty Ninth Entry:

Okay, so you know how sometimes I go to the Wednesday EA meetings? Well I went today and man am I ever glad I did. I learned about another kind of depression. Two actually.

The first one is - Dysthymia. This is a type of depression that causes you to be in low moods for a really long period of time, like this can last over years.

The man who spoke about having this depression today said that this depression is usually easier to talk about then take medicine for. Because it goes on for such a long time, he said that was just his opinion though. And people with Dysthymia are at risk for episodes of Major Depressive Disorder.

The second one is - Adjustment Disorder /or Situational Depression. This one is triggered by stressful events in your life, like death, trauma, being fired from jobs, break ups, etc.

The woman who runs the EA meetings spoke about this depression and she told us a lot about it. She said that this depression is about 3-4 times more common than Major Depression. Though it is different in the way that medication is rarely needed because it usually clears up after whatever tragic event has passed for the person. Even though it goes away after upsetting events, it shouldn't be ignored. And that's why she runs these meetings. To keep the awareness out there. Especially for people suffering from this type of depression because they're signs may become warning to the person having Major Depression.

Wow! This is crazy. It never ceases to amaze me about the different types and levels to the types of depression there is out there. It makes me want to spread the awareness to others that much more. I just think everyone should at least have the basic knowledge of the different types. I'm not saying they need to become activists or anything like that. But just to have a better understanding of how to interact with people who suffer with depression. I feel like if people knew the basics then it'd be easier to communicate. And in hope, maybe it would help the depressed people be more open to sharing. Because the people they thought hated them, actually never hated them, they just didn't know how to act around them. Maybe they just didn't want to say the wrong thing to upset the depressed person even more. Who knows! But you'll never know unless you try right?!

That's why I want to help people so bad. I know what it's like first hand for a lot of this stuff. I want to be able to look back at my life when I'm older and say I made a difference in people's lives. I was the reason they started to follow their dreams instead of hiding in their bedrooms barely keeping themselves together. I want to be the reason young men and women have the confidence in themselves to achieve absolutely everything and anything they set their minds to.

I made the change in my life. Hell we all know I'm not perfect. I know I'll never get there either. But I'm learning to love myself and I think that's what matters the most. Because at the end of each day, it's just me laying there in my bed. No one else. With self doubt I start to dig too deep into situations that I don't need to. I over think way too much. But. By learning to love myself. Love my scars. I'm beginning to realize that I am good enough. Good enough for anything that I set my mind to do. And God knows I will achieve everything I set out to do. I've come a hell of a long way. And I have got an even longer road ahead of me. But you know what. I'm looking forward to it.

Yours Truly,

Abigail Mitchell

Hi wow! It's been crazy busy the past few days, but today is the day!

PROM! I'm so excited and so nervous at the same time.

Man I was so concerned I wasn't going to find the perfect dress, but yesterday my sister and I just went to the mall to pick up her dry cleaning and I saw this amazing dress next door. It's this beautiful royal blue color, floor length and it has some silver beading on the front! And the best news… It was on sale! Yay! I don't have very good luck, but when it comes to sales, I'm the girl to go with to find the best ones! I don't know what it is, it's like they just know I'm coming!

Anyway! I'm home now getting ready. My sister, mom and of course Alex are helping me. I literally have done nothing all day! I love it. Ha! Alex did my makeup, my mom is now doing my hair and my sis is painting my toe nails. So I've got time to journal! I had to squeeze just a bit of an entry because it's been a few days and I'm just so excited! I've resorted to sharing my excitement here with you because I think I've overdone it with everyone else (insert evil laugh here, tehehe!). And I would rather my mom not put the bobby pins into my skull so I think this is my best option!

After we're done getting ready Dylan is going to pick me up and we're going to see Lexi at the hospital before going to the school. Lexi is getting dressed up too. She insisted she wanted to be a part of our prom pictures even if she has tubes sticking out of her. She's

12 going on 32 I swear! How can you not love that girl though. And I wouldn't want it any other way. She's a part of my family, so she's a part of this beautiful day too.

On a more serious note, I'm kind of really nervous to show up tonight… I mean, I haven't really seen anyone since, well, you know. I'm not sure how they'll react to seeing me. I hope they're nice. But like genuine nice, not the fake nice because they have to be nice to you. Oh well, we'll see I guess… You know, the more I think about it, the more I don't really care. Tonight shouldn't be about that. It's about prom, it's about Dylan and I, it's about being happy in my own skin.

My *scarred* skin. Ugh…

My dress doesn't have sleeves… When I went to school I usually wore long sleeve shirts or cardigans or something to cover up my scars. And now they're going to be out in the open for everyone to see… Everyone that I haven't seen in a few months… Now get to see everything about me… Wow…

No.

You know what, no. No! I don't care. I have come too far to back out now. I have scars. SO WHAT. I'm only human. Looking in the mirror as my mom finishes my hair… I feel beautiful. No one can take this night away from me. No one.

I can do this. No need to wish me luck tonight journal.

Maybe wish my graduating class luck… How they're going to handle all this hotness I do not know! HAHA totally kidding. At least I can still make myself laugh.

Yours Truly,

Abigail Mitchell

The Big Day

Abigail was putting the finishing touches to her hair when the doorbell rang. It was Dylan, all dressed up in his black tuxedo, and gorgeous corsage to match Abi's dress. Mrs. Mitchell stopped him in the doorway to take a few pictures. Then his jaw dropped. Abigail was coming down the staircase and the once chatty living room was now so silent you could hear a pin drop.

"My baby girl is all grown up," cried her mother.

"That's not my little girl! Hi, hello. Yes, has anyone seen Abigail Melanie?" joked her father.

Speechless, trying to find something to say, Dylan finally says, "I… I think I'm the luckiest guy in the world. Wow Abi, you are simply stunning."

"Okay guys stop," Abigail blushes, "We're going to be late if we don't leave now, I want as much time with Lexi as possible before the dance."

"Not before I get my pictures!" Mrs. Mitchell hugged her daughter. The whole family gathered around, one by one taking pictures with Abigail and Dylan. After about ten minutes trying to get the tripod and timer set on the camera, they finally got a group shot. With hugs finishing up by the door, one last picture of Abigail and her parents. "We love you Abigail, sweetheart. Stay safe and have fun tonight. Call us if you need anything."

And like that, Abigail and Dylan left to go to the prom.

"First stop, Lexi!"

"Actually Abs, I have one more surprise for you before we go," smiled Dylan. Out of the glove compartment he pulled out a bag. Abigail opened it up to the most beautiful earrings she had ever seen. Silver hoops to match her dress. But how did he know? Abigail thought. No need to ask… Lexi. Of course.

Abigail and Dylan got to the hospital in plenty of time. Lexi was already waiting for them. She looked like herself again. That one afternoon Abigail and her mother brought wigs to the hospital to play dress up with, turns out there was one that was almost exact same to Lexi's haircut before she lost all her hair. And tonight she was wearing it, proudly. Mr. Michaels was almost as bad as Mrs. Mitchell with pictures. Prom only happens once, and since Mrs. Michaels passing, the family has let nothing take away from their happiness.

It was time for Abigail and Dylan to leave. As they were saying their goodbyes Abigail gave Lexi a little present of her own. Her journal. There still was hundreds of empty pages waiting to be written on, but Abigail felt her time had passed and it was time for a new author. Lexi. "It will listen with no judgment. Just like me, always." Shocked and touched, Lexi accepted the journal and promised to take good care of it.

***

At the dance Abigail had the time of her life. No one laughed at her, no one called her names, they were nice to her. They might have just been doing it out of pity or guilt but they were doing it and that's all that really mattered to Abigail.

And they danced, literally like there was no tomorrow. Abigail wore the brightest smile anyone had ever saw. She was so beautiful and genuinely happy, without knowing her you'd never know she was depressed. And for all she cared, at that moment, she wasn't depressed. She was normal. She was a teenage girl at her high school prom with her boyfriend whom she loved. She was herself. She was happy.

Abigail started making plans with some of the girls that were on the soccer team, to hangout over summer break. They also agreed to come to her birthday party this year. They were laughing to the point of tears, happy tears. And Dylan just watched. He watched as the love of his young life shined so bright without even trying.

"God, I love you," whispered Dylan to himself.

"What's that sweetheart?" Asked Abigail.

"Nothing Abs," he blushed.

The last dance was to a slow song, one from the mix-tape Abigail made for Dylan last year. It's the little things she thought, smiling to herself. As they were getting ready to leave, Abigail said goodbye to her friends while Dylan got their coats.

"Excuse me! Can I please get everyone's attention." A familiar voice came from the microphone on the stage. It was Abigail's Principle. "As you guys and gals know this is my last year as your principle and I wanted to make one last announcement to you all while we are still here together. All of you know we lost a great young man this year James. I just wanted to remind the returning classes that even though I won't be your principle next year, and to the graduates, my phone is always on me. A phone call or email away and I'll be there for my students. Because once an Eagle always an Eagle!" The crowd of students up roared in applause and cheers. After that the students took their last pictures as they headed off in different directions.

***

"So you had a good time, sweetie?"

"Yes!" her eyes sparkled with joy. "I had the best time tonight." Abigail said as they drove away from the school to head home.

"Do you want to stop for a milkshake?" Dylan asked, hoping she'd say yes just so he could spend even more time with her, because she had never looked so beautiful to him. Not just because she was all dressed up. But because she was happy, she didn't care about anything but the moment they were in. He didn't want that night to end.

"Oh my gosh, yes I'd love to!"

Dylan put his blinker on to turn onto the highway. The best milkshake place was just a few kilometers down the highway away from their school. The two were smiling ear to ear, singing along to the radio without a care in the world.

And the it all went black.

After the Darkness

Sirens filled his head, flashing lights blurred in front of him. Dylan woke up on a stretcher being lifted into an ambulance. Unsure of what was going on, Dylan starting mumbling into screams.

"Abi. Where is Abigail? My girlfriend… Abigail! Hello! Where is she? She was right next to me."

"Sir please calm down, breathe. We are taking you to St. John's Hospital. You've just been in a car accident. Can you please spell out your full name and birth-date for me." Said the young EMT.

"I want to know where Abigail is. Forget about me. She needs my help. Abigail!"

"Sir please-"

"Dylan, my name is Dylan Michaels can you please tell me where she is, she was in the passenger seat. Is she okay? Why can't I see her? Where is she? Where did you take her? Will she be at the hospital too? Is she already there? Is she okay? Please I need to know that she is okay. Where is she?"

"Mitchell, Abigail. That's your girlfriend? We found her I.D. in her clutch."

"Yes, that's her."

"We did all we could but she died on contact. The airbag was to strong compared to her little body. Her neck suffered too many fractions and the right side of her face was deeply cut with glass. There was nothing we could of done when we got here. I'm sorry."

Completely speechless, Dylan fell silent. He couldn't bring himself to speak, but his brain was going insane with questions. She was gone? Just like that? But we just left the prom. We were singing our favourite song. We were laughing. We were going for milkshakes. How was this possible? She was right next to him. Why did she die instantly and not him? Airbags are supposed to save people, not kill them! If he hadn't suggested going for milkshakes this wouldn't of happened. It was his fault. His. He just wanted to spend one more hour with her before taking her home. They were happy, she was happy. And now she's gone. She's dead.

The ambulance doors shut and they drove off. Dylan was being hooked up to an IV and Abigail was dead. That's all Dylan could think. She was dead. He was alive. Abigail was gone.

The Next Morning

The Michaels were sitting around Dylan's bed waiting for him to wake up. Flowers, balloons and cookies were spread out on his bedside table. After a while Dylan awoke with a scream, "ABIGAIL."

"Dylan, Dylan breathe. Please. It's okay. It was just a nightmare. You're okay." Mr. Michaels tried to comfort his son.

Catching his breath, "Please tell me she's not actually gone. Please." Tears filled his eyes and poured down his face, unable to hear his fathers answer.

Unsure how to respond, he took a breath and said, "Son, I'm sorry."

"I'm sure she was the happiest she has ever been, Dyl. She probably had the biggest smile on her face. At least she was happy. You made her happy, please remember that. She loved you. She-"

"JUST STOP," he yelled.

The room fell silent. You could feel the guilt in the air. Dylan knew it was his fault. If he just took her home. Had ice cream from her freezer rather than milkshakes. It was his fault. That's all he could think. This whole thing was his fault.

"Dylan you cannot blame yourself, the accident was not even your fault. It was the other vehicles'. You are not to blame here. The other driver was charged with drunk driving. You cannot blame this on yourself Dylan, it was not your fault. Please, son." Mr. Michaels tried explaining to his son.

"It was my fault, I suggested milkshakes. We wouldn't of been on the highway if it wasn't for me. I just wanted to spend a little more time with her. She just looked so beautiful."

99

Heartbroken Mr. Michaels replied, "Dylan, breathe, please. Ok, it was not your fault. You cannot beat yourself up over this."

"How can I not?! I'm alive and she is not. I was driving, she was not. If it wasn't for me…"

The room was silent. The nurse came in to check Dylan's vitals. No one said a word until she left. Lexi sensed they should just give him some time. So her and her dad left to go get some food from the cafeteria.

Dylan was left alone with his thoughts. And man, they were all over the place in his head. He couldn't think straight. All he could think was Abigail was gone. The love of his life. His seventeen year old life partner was gone. And Dylan. He was left alive to live without her. They had fought before sure, arguments saying they would rather see the other person die. But neither of them meant it. No one ever means that in arguments. And when they'd make up, they would say they couldn't live without each other. But, now, Dylan had to. How was he supposed to live without her? They had a routine. It was almost her birthday. He already had her gift. He had everything planned out. And now, nothing.

Later that day the Mitchell's came to visit Dylan in the hospital. After giving Dylan hugs no one spoke for what felt like ages. No one knew what to say or if they should even say anything. Everyone knew it wasn't Dylan's fault. It was a drunk driver. But still, Abigail was gone and the Mitchell's wanted to blame it on someone. But seeing Dylan laying there in pain, broken arm and leg. They couldn't.

The Memorial

A week after the accident they held Abigail's funeral at the church near their house. Standing room only, the Mitchell's were overwhelmed with support. Their youngest daughter was gone, but they weren't alone.

Pictures of Abigail filled the hall after the ceremony. There was lunch set out for all the guests. People were chatting, a few tears were shed, and strangely some laughter was shared. Dylan was in a wheelchair but that wasn't going to stop him from being there today. There were people from the EA meetings, Abigail's therapist, students from her high school (students Dylan didn't even think knew Abigail, but he was glad to see the immense amount of support).

"…Abigail may of felt like she was alone sometimes, but she wasn't. I would of never imagined a turn out like this, but I'm not really surprised. Abi was an amazing girl who affected everyone she met. Some of you knew about her depression and some of you didn't. But that didn't matter, because she always managed to be able to make us all laugh in one way or the other." Dylan paused before continuing, "Today she would want us to smile and laugh. No tears, trust me she knew what it was to be sad, and she absolutely hated to see anyone she cared about upset. Even if she was going through something worse, it didn't matter, you mattered more. She would put her problems aside to help you. So that her full attention was on you. A beautiful face, heart and soul. So when you remember Abigail, please remember her big smile and contagious laugh. She would appreciate it."

Cheers and applause blew over Dylan. People crowded around him, offering their condolences and best wishes for a full recovery. The principle of their high school even showed up. "Mr. Michaels, Dylan, and Lexi," he hugged each one, then continued, "I just spoke with Abigail's family. Mr. and Mrs. Mitchell have agreed to building a small memorial in Abigail's name to be placed outside the school's general office. I hope that you all will be there on graduation day, as we plan to reveal it then. With your permission I would like to involve you as well, Dylan. You see, you have a greater affect to your fellow peers than you realize." He offered a smile, "Take your time and think about it. But please let me know once you've decided. I'd love to have you up there with me on stage to reveal a beautiful memorial for an even more special young lady. My condolences."

Group by group the crowd started thinning out. The photographs were being put back into boxes, flower vases getting carefully packed up and plates of food being given away to everyone leaving. It was over. Abigail's body was now in the ground. People from all over came to offer their support to the Mitchell's. They truly were not alone, even though they sure felt it.

It's a shame. Mr. Mitchell thought, "If only a third of these people showed a little more interest in our Abigail… Maybe, maybe she'd still be here today." And just like that the SUV was packed up as they drove away from the church.

Hi Journal. It's Lexi, I guess I'm your new owner now. Abigail gave you to me. I actually forgot about it for a while, but I was going through some things in my room and came across it. I remember Abi giving this to me. Like it was yesterday. But it wasn't. It's already been a month since she's been gone… It's really hard to believe.

Abs looked so beautiful the last time I saw her, their prom night and honestly that how I'll always remember her. Like a big sister. My big sister. I'll always remember her saying how much she believed in me, and how if she could get out of bed every day, then so could I. Abigail Melanie Mitchell was and forever will be an angel. I know she was depressed but it never seemed to come up when she was around me. She cared more about making me laugh and smile, than she did about herself. Even though she was going through things, it was never a topic between us. She always wanted to make me happy. To be honest, I kind of wish she would of talked to me about some of her thoughts though. I don't know how much help I could have been, but I can't help but think that I could have been there, yenno.

I think that's why she gave me her journal though. I remember her saying "It will listen with no judgment, like me, always." All of her entries are still in here. Maybe I'll read through them one day, but I'm just not ready for that I don't think. Not yet at least. I think I might give it to Dyl to read. Maybe it'll help him out.

He's not doing well at all. He still blames himself, I can't blame him, no one can.

Mrs. Mitchell still comes over to the house every week to see me. Even with Abigail being gone. You know I always thought it was only because Abi wanted to visit me in the hospital that her mom came too. But still Mrs. Mitchell continues to come. And honestly, it's a little difficult. But so comforting, and soothing. No one could ever replace my mom, but to have another figure there when needed really does take a little bit off.

It's tough not having Abigail around, I guess we're all just trying to do our best to cope.

Well until next time.

Lexi Michaels<3

CPSIA information can be obtained
at www.ICGtesting.com
Printed in the USA
LVHW091733050119
602837LV00002BA/148/P